KU-299-137

COSMOPOLIS

ALSO BY DON DeLILLO

COSMOPOLIS

DON DeLILLO

PICADOR

MORAY COUNCIL
LIBRARIES &
INFO.SERVICES

2O 11 59 14

Askews

F

First published 2003 by Scribner,
a division of Simon & Schuster, Inc., New York

This edition published 2003 by Picador
an imprint of Pan Macmillan Ltd
Pan Macmillan, 20 New Wharf Road, London N1 9RR
Basingstoke and Oxford
Associated companies throughout the world
www.panmacmillan.com

ISBN 0 330 41276 0

Copyright © Don DeLillo 2003

The right of Don DeLillo to be identified as the
author of this work has been asserted by him in accordance
with the Copyright, Designs and Patents Act 1988.

All rights reserved. No part of this publication may be
reproduced, stored in or introduced into a retrieval system, or
transmitted, in any form, or by any means (electronic, mechanical,
photocopying, recording or otherwise) without the prior written
permission of the publisher. Any person who does any unauthorized
act in relation to this publication may be liable to criminal
prosecution and civil claims for damages.

1 3 5 7 9 8 6 4 2

A CIP catalogue record for this book is available from
the British Library.

Printed and bound in Great Britain by
Mackays of Chatham plc, Chatham, Kent

To Paul Auster

a rat became the unit of currency

ZBIGNIEW HERBERT

COSMOPOLIS

IN THE YEAR
2000

A Day in April

PART ONE

1

Sleep failed him more often now, not once or twice a week but four times, five. What did he do when this happened? He did not take long walks into the scrolling dawn. There was no friend he loved enough to harrow with a call. What was there to say? It was a matter of silences, not words.

He tried to read his way into sleep but only grew more wakeful. He read science and poetry. He liked spare poems sited minutely in white space, ranks of alphabetic strokes burnt into paper. Poems made him conscious of his breathing. A poem bared the moment to things he was not normally prepared to notice. This was the nuance of every poem, at least for him, at night, these long weeks, one breath after another, in the rotating room at the top of the triplex.

He tried to sleep standing up one night, in his meditation cell, but wasn't nearly adept enough, monk enough to manage this. He bypassed sleep and rounded into counterpoise, a moonless calm in which every force is balanced by another. This was the briefest of easings, a small pause in the stir of restless identities.

There was no answer to the question. He tried sedatives and hypnotics but they made him dependent, sending him inward in tight spirals. Every act he performed was self-haunted and synthetic. The palest thought carried an anxious shadow. What did he do? He did not consult an analyst in a tall leather chair. Freud is finished, Einstein's next. He was reading the Special Theory tonight, in English and German, but put the book aside, finally, and lay completely still, trying to summon the will to speak the single word that would turn off the lights. Nothing existed around him. There was only the noise in his head, the mind in time.

When he died he would not end. The world would end.

He stood at the window and watched the great day dawn. The view was across bridges, narrows and sounds and out past the boroughs and toothpaste suburbs into measures of landmass and sky that could only be called the deep distance. He didn't know what he wanted. It was still nighttime down on the river, half night, and ashy vapors wavered above the smokestacks on the far bank. He imagined the whores were all fled from the lamplit corners by now, duck butts shaking, other kinds of archaic business just beginning to stir, produce trucks rolling out of the markets, news trucks out of the loading docks. The bread vans would be crossing the city and a few stray cars out of bedlam weaving down the avenues, speakers pumping heavy sound.

The noblest thing, a bridge across a river, with the sun beginning to roar behind it.

He watched a hundred gulls trail a wobbling scow downriver. They had large strong hearts. He knew this, disproportionate to body size. He'd been interested once and had mastered the teeming details of bird anatomy. Birds have hollow bones. He mastered the steepest matters in half an afternoon.

He didn't know what he wanted. Then he knew. He wanted to get a haircut.

He stood a while longer, watching a single gull lift and ripple in a furl of air, admiring the bird, thinking into it, trying to know the bird, feeling the sturdy earnest beat of its scavenger's ravenous heart.

He wore a suit and tie. A suit subdued the camber of his overdeveloped chest. He liked to work out at night, pulling weighted metal sleds, doing curls and bench presses in stoic repetitions that ate away the day's tumults and compulsions.

He walked through the apartment, forty-eight rooms. He did this when he felt hesitant and depressed, striding past the lap pool, the card parlor, the gymnasium, past the shark tank and screening room. He stopped at the borzoi pen and talked to his dogs. Then he went to the annex, where there were currencies to track and research reports to examine.

The yen rose overnight against expectations.

He went back up to the living quarters, walking slowly now, and paused in every room, absorbing what was there, deeply seeing, retaining every fleck of energy in rays and waves.

The art that hung was mainly color-field and geometric, large canvases that dominated rooms and placed a prayerful hush on the atrium, skylighted, with its high white paintings and trickle fountain. The atrium had the tension and suspense of a towering space that requires pious silence in order to be seen and experienced properly, the mosque of soft footfall and rock doves murmurous in the vaulting.

He liked paintings that his guests did not know how to look at. The white paintings were unknowable to many, knife-applied slabs of mucoid color. The work was all the more dangerous for not being new. There's no more danger in the new.

He rode to the marble lobby in the elevator that played Satie. His prostate was asymmetrical. He went outside and crossed the avenue, then turned and faced the building where he lived. He felt contiguous with it. It was eighty-nine stories, a prime number, in an undistinguished sheath of hazy bronze glass. They shared an edge or boundary, skyscraper and man. It was nine hundred feet high, the tallest residential tower in the world, a commonplace oblong whose only statement was its size. It had the kind of banality that reveals itself over time as being truly brutal. He

8

liked it for this reason. He liked to stand and look at it when he felt this way. He felt wary, drowsy and insubstantial.

The wind came cutting off the river. He took out his hand organizer and poked a note to himself about the anachronistic quality of the word skyscraper. No recent structure ought to bear this word. It belonged to the olden soul of awe, to the arrowed towers that were a narrative long before he was born.

The hand device itself was an object whose original culture had just about disappeared. He knew he'd have to junk it.

The tower gave him strength and depth. He knew what he wanted, a haircut, but stood a while longer in the soaring noise of the street and studied the mass and scale of the tower. The one virtue of its surface was to skim and bend the river light and mime the tides of open sky. There was an aura of texture and reflection. He scanned its length and felt connected to it, sharing the surface and the environment that came into contact with the surface, from both sides. A surface separates inside from out and belongs no less to one than the other. He'd thought about surfaces in the shower once.

He put on his sunglasses. Then he walked back across the avenue and approached the lines of white limousines. There were ten cars, five in a curbside row in front of the tower, on First Avenue, and five lined up on the cross street, facing west. The cars were identical at a glance. Some may have been a foot or two longer than others depending on details of the stretch work and the particular owner's requirements.

The drivers smoked and talked on the sidewalk, hatless in dark suits, sharing an alertness that would be evident only in retrospect when their eyes went hot in their heads and they shed their cigarettes and vacated their unstudied stances, having spotted the objects of their regard.

For now they talked, in accented voices, some of them, or first languages, others, and they waited for the investment banker, the land developer, the venture capitalist, for the software entrepreneur, the global overlord of satellite and cable, the discount broker, the beaked media chief, for the exiled head of state of some smashed landscape of famine and war.

In the park across the street there were stylized ironwork arbors and bronze fountains with iridescent pennies scattershot at the bottom. A man in women's clothing walked seven elegant dogs.

He liked the fact that the cars were indistinguishable from each other. He wanted such a car because he thought it was a platonic replica, weightless for all its size, less an object than an idea. But he knew this wasn't true. This was something he said for effect and he didn't believe it for an instant. He believed it for an instant but only just. He wanted the car because it was not only oversized but aggressively and contemptuously so, metastasizingly so, a tremendous mutant thing that stood astride every argument against it.

His chief of security liked the car for its anonymity.

10

Long white limousines had become the most unnoticed vehicles in the city. He was waiting on the sidewalk now, Torval, bald and no-necked, a man whose head seemed removable for maintenance.

"Where?" he said.

"I want a haircut."

"The president's in town."

"We don't care. We need a haircut. We need to go crosstown."

"You will hit traffic that speaks in quarter inches."

"Just so I know. Which president are we talking about?"

"United States. Barriers will be set up," he said. "Entire streets deleted from the map."

"Show me my car," he told the man.

The driver held the door open, ready to jog around the rear of the car and down to his own door, thirty-five feet away. Where the file of white limousines ended, parallel to the entrance of the Japan Society, another line of cars commenced, the town cars, black or indigo, and the drivers waited for members of diplomatic missions, for the delegates, consuls and sunglassed attachés.

Torval sat with the driver up front, where there were dashboard computer screens and a night-vision display on the lower windshield, a product of the infrared camera situated in the grille.

Shiner was waiting inside the car, his chief of technology, small and boy-faced. He did not look at Shiner anymore. He hadn't looked in three years. Once you'd looked, there was nothing else to know. You'd know his bone

11

marrow in a beaker. He wore his faded shirt and jeans and sat in his masturbatory crouch.

"What have we learned then?"

"Our system's secure. We're impenetrable. There's no rogue program," Shiner said.

"It would seem, however."

"Eric, no. We ran every test. Nobody's overloading the system or manipulating our sites."

"When did we do all this?"

"Yesterday. At the complex. Our rapid-response team. There's no vulnerable point of entry. Our insurer did a threat analysis. We're buffered from attack."

"Everywhere."

"Yes."

"Including the car."

"Including, absolutely, yes."

"My car. This car."

"Eric, yes, please."

"We've been together, you and I, since the little bitty start-up. I want you to tell me that you still have the stamina to do this job. The single-mindedness."

"This car. Your car."

"The relentless will. Because I keep hearing about our legend. We're all young and smart and were raised by wolves. But the phenomenon of reputation is a delicate thing. A person rises on a word and falls on a syllable. I know I'm asking the wrong man."

"What?"

"Where was the car last night after we ran our tests?"

"I don't know."

"Where do all these limos go at night?"

Shiner slumped hopelessly into the depths of this question.

"I know I'm changing the subject. I haven't been sleeping much. I look at books and drink brandy. But what happens to all the stretch limousines that prowl the throbbing city all day long? Where do they spend the night?"

The car ran into stalled traffic before it reached Second Avenue. He sat in the club chair at the rear of the cabin looking into the array of visual display units. There were medleys of data on every screen, all the flowing symbols and alpine charts, the polychrome numbers pulsing. He absorbed this material in a couple of long still seconds, ignoring the speech sounds that issued from lacquered heads. There was a microwave and a heart monitor. He looked at the spycam on a swivel and it looked back at him. He used to sit here in hand-held space but that was finished now. The context was nearly touchless. He could talk most systems into operation or wave a hand at a screen and make it go blank.

A cab squeezed in alongside, the driver pressing his horn. This set off a hundred other horns.

Shiner stirred in the jump seat near the liquor cabinet, facing rearward. He was drinking fresh orange juice through a plastic straw that extended from the glass at an obtuse angle. He seemed to be whistling something into the shaft of the straw between intakes of liquid.

Eric said, "What?"

Shiner raised his head.

"Do you get the feeling sometimes that you don't know what's going on?" he said.

"Do I want to ask what you mean by that?"

Shiner spoke into his straw as if it were an onboard implement of transmission.

"All this optimism, all this booming and soaring. Things happen like bang. This and that simultaneous. I put out my hand and what do I feel? I know there's a thousand things you analyze every ten minutes. Patterns, ratios, indexes, whole maps of information. I love information. This is our sweetness and light. It's a fuckall wonder. And we have meaning in the world. People eat and sleep in the shadow of what we do. But at the same time, what?"

There was a long pause. He looked at Shiner finally. What did he say to the man? He did not direct a remark that was hard and sharp. He said nothing at all in fact.

They sat in the swell of blowing horns. There was something about the noise that he did not choose to wish away. It was the tone of some fundamental ache, a lament so old it sounded aboriginal. He thought of men in shaggy bands bellowing ceremonially, social units established to kill and eat. Red meat. That was the call, the grievous need. The cooler carried beverages today. There was nothing solid for the microwave.

Shiner said, "Any special reason we're in the car instead of the office?"

"How do you know we're in the car instead of the office?"

"If I answer that question."

"Based on what premise?"

"I know I'll say something that's halfway clever but mostly shallow and probably inaccurate on some level. Then you'll pity me for having been born."

"We're in the car because I need a haircut."

"Have the barber go to the office. Get your haircut there. Or have the barber come to the car. Get your haircut and go to the office."

"A haircut has what. Associations. Calendar on the wall. Mirrors everywhere. There's no barber chair here. Nothing swivels but the spycam."

He shifted position in his chair and watched the surveillance camera adjust. His image used to be accessible nearly all the time, videostreamed worldwide from the car, the plane, the office and selected sites in his apartment. But there were security issues to address and now the camera operated on a closed circuit. A nurse and two armed guards were on constant watch at three monitors in a windowless room at the office. The word office was outdated now. It had zero saturation.

He glanced out the one-way window to his left. It took him a moment to understand that he knew the woman in the rear seat of the taxi that lay adjacent. She was his wife of twenty-two days, Elise Shifrin, a poet who had right of blood to the fabulous Shifrin banking fortune of Europe and the world.

He coded a word to Torval up front. Then he stepped into the street and tapped on the taxi window. She smiled up at him, surprised. She was in her mid-twenties, with an etched delicacy of feature and large and artless eyes. Her beauty had an element of remoteness. This was intriguing but maybe not. Her head rode slightly forward on a slender length of neck. She had an unexpected laugh, a little weary and experienced, and he liked the way she put a finger to her lips when she wanted to be thoughtful. Her poetry was shit.

She slid over and he got in next to her. The horns subsided and resumed in ritualistic cycles. Then the taxi shot diagonally across the intersection to a point just west of Second Avenue, where it reached another impasse, with Torval jogging hot behind.

"Where's your car?"

"We can't seem to find it," she said.

"I'd offer you a ride."

"I couldn't. Absolutely. I know you work en route. And I like taxis. I was never good at geography and I learn things by asking the drivers where they come from."

"They come from horror and despair."

"Yes, exactly. One learns about the countries where unrest is occurring by riding the taxis here."

"I haven't seen you in a while. I looked for you this morning."

He took off his sunglasses, for effect. She gazed into his face. She looked steadily, with fixed attention.

"Your eyes are blue," she said.

He lifted her hand and held it to his face, smelling and licking. The Sikh at the wheel was missing a finger. Eric regarded the stub, impressive, a serious thing, a body ruin that carried history and pain.

"Eat breakfast yet?"

"No," she said.

"Good. I'm hungry for something thick and chewy."

"You never told me you were blue-eyed."

He heard the static in her laugh. He bit her thumb knuckle and opened the door and they stepped across the sidewalk to the coffee shop near the corner.

He sat with his back to the wall, watching Torval position himself near the front door, where he had a broad view of the room. The place was crowded. He heard stray words in French and Somali seeping through the ambient noise. That was the disposition of this end of 47th Street. Dark women in ivory robes walking in the river wind toward the UN secretariat. Apartment towers called L'Ecole and Octavia. There were Irish nannies pushing strollers in the parks. And Elise of course, Swiss or something, sitting across the table.

"What are we going to talk about?" she said.

He sat before a plate of pancakes and sausages, waiting for the square of butter to melt and run so he could use his fork to swirl it into the torpid syrup and then watch the marks made by the tines slowly fold into the soak. He realized her question was serious.

"We want a heliport on the roof. I've acquired air

rights but still need to get a zoning variance. Don't you want to eat?"

It seemed, the food, to make her draw back. Green tea and toast untouched before her.

"And a shooting range next to the elevator bank. Let's talk about us."

"You and I. We're here. So might as well."

"When are we going to have sex again?"

"We will. I promise," she said.

"We haven't in a while now."

"When I work, you see. The energy is precious."

"When you write."

"Yes."

"Where do you do this? I look for you, Elise."

He watched Torval move his lips thirty feet away. He was speaking into a mouthpiece concealed in his lapel. He wore an ear bud. The handset of his cell phone was belted under his jacket not far from his voice-activated firearm, Czech-made, another emblem of the international tenor of the district.

"I curl up somewhere. I've always done this. My mother used to send people to find me," she said. "Maids and gardeners combing the house and grounds. She thought I was dissolvable in water."

"I like your mother. You have your mother's breasts."

"Her breasts."

"Great stand-up tits," he said.

He ate quickly, inhaling his food. Then he ate her food. He thought he could feel the glucose entering his cells, fueling the body's other appetites. He nodded to the owner of the place, a Greek from Samos, who waved from the counter. He liked to come here because Torval did not want him to.

"Tell me this. Where will you go now?" she said. "To a meeting somewhere? To your office? Where is your office? What do you do exactly?"

She peered at him over bridged hands, her smile in hiding.

"You know things. I think this is what you do," she said. "I think you're dedicated to knowing. I think you acquire information and turn it into something stupendous and awful. You're a dangerous person. Do you agree? A visionary."

He watched Torval bend a hand to the side of his head, listening to the person who was speaking into his ear bud. He knew these devices were already vestigial. They were degenerate structures. Maybe not the handgun just yet. But the word itself was lost in blowing mist.

He stood by the car, parked illegally, and listened to Torval.

"Report from the complex. There's a credible threat. Not to be dismissed. This means a ride crosstown."

"We've had numerous threats. All credible. I'm still standing here."

"Not a threat to your safety. To his."

"Who the fuck is his?"

"The president's. This means a ride crosstown does not happen unless we make a day of it, with cookies and milk."

19

He found that Torval's burly presence was a provocation. He was knotted and sloped. He had the body of a heavy lifter, appearing to stand and squat simultaneously. His bearing was one of blunt persuasion, with the earnest alertness that thickset men bring to a task. These were hostile incitements. They engaged Eric's sense of his own physical authority, his standards of force and brawn.

"Do people still shoot at presidents? I thought there were more stimulating targets," he said.

He looked for steady temperament in his security staff. Torval did not match the pattern. Times he was ironic and other times faintly disdainful of standard procedures. Then there was his head. There was something in the jut of his shaved head and the aberrant set of his eyes that carried an inference of abiding anger. His job was to be selective in his terms of confrontation, not hate a faceless world.

He'd noticed that Torval had stopped calling him Mr. Packer. He called him nothing now. This omission left a space in nature large enough for a man to walk through.

He realized Elise was gone. He'd forgotten to ask where she was headed.

"In the next block there are two haircutting salons. One, two," Torval said. "No need to go crosstown. The situation isn't stable."

People hurried past, the others of the street, endless anonymous, twenty-one lives per second, race-walking in their faces and pigments, sprays of fleetest being.

They were here to make the point that you did not have to look at them.

Michael Chin was in the jump seat now, his currency analyst, calmly modeling a certain sizable disquiet.

"I know that smile, Michael."

"I think the yen. I mean there's reason to believe we may be leveraging too rashly."

"It's going to turn our way."

"Yes. I know. It always has."

"The rashness you think you see."

"What is happening doesn't chart."

"It charts. You have to search a little harder. Don't trust standard models. Think outside the limits. The yen is making a statement. Read it. Then leap."

"We are betting big-time here."

"I know that smile. I want to respect it. But the yen can't go any higher."

"We are borrowing enormous, enormous sums."

"Any assault on the borders of perception is going to seem rash at first."

"Eric, come on. We are speculating into the void."

"Your mother blamed the smile on your father. He blamed her. There's something deathly about it."

"I think we ought to adjust."

"She thought she'd have to enroll you in special counseling."

Chin had advanced degrees in mathematics and economics and was only a kid, still, with a gutterpunk stripe in his hair, a moody beet-root red.

The two men talked and made decisions. These were Eric's decisions, which Chin entered resentfully in his hand organizer and then synched with the system. The car was moving. Eric watched himself on the oval screen below the spycam, running his thumb along his chinline. The car stopped and moved and he realized queerly that he'd just placed his thumb on his chinline, a second or two after he'd seen it on-screen.

"Where is Shiner?"

"On his way to the airport."

"Why do we still have airports? Why are they called airports?"

"I know I can't answer these questions without losing your respect," Chin said.

"Shiner told me our network is secure."

"Then it is."

"Safe from penetration."

"He's the best there is at finding holes."

"Then why am I seeing things that haven't happened yet?"

The floor of the limousine was Carrara marble, from the quarries where Michelangelo stood half a millennium ago, touching the tip of his finger to the starry white stone.

He looked at Chin, adrift in his jump seat, lost in rambling thought.

22

"How old are you?"

"Twenty-two. What? Twenty-two."

"You look younger. I was always younger than anyone around me. One day it began to change."

"I don't feel younger. I feel located totally nowhere. I think I'm ready to quit, basically, the business."

"Put a stick of gum in your mouth and try not to chew it. For someone your age, with your gifts, there's only one thing in the world worth pursuing professionally and intellectually. What is it, Michael? The interaction between technology and capital. The inseparability."

"High school was the last true challenge," Chin said.

The car drifted into gridlock on Third Avenue. The driver's standing orders were to advance into blocked intersections, not hang feebly back.

"There's a poem I read in which a rat becomes the unit of currency."

"Yes. That would be interesting," Chin said.

"Yes. That would impact the world economy."

"The name alone. Better than the dong or the kwacha."

"The name says everything."

"Yes. The rat," Chin said.

"Yes. The rat closed lower today against the euro."

"Yes. There is growing concern that the Russian rat will be devalued."

"White rats. Think about that."

"Yes. Pregnant rats."

"Yes. Major sell-off of pregnant Russian rats."

"Britain converts to the rat," Chin said.

"Yes. Joins trend to universal currency."

"Yes. U.S. establishes rat standard."

"Yes. Every U.S. dollar redeemable for rat."

"Dead rats."

"Yes. Stockpiling of dead rats called global health menace."

"How old are you?" Chin said. "Now that you're not younger than everyone else."

He looked past Chin toward streams of numbers running in opposite directions. He understood how much it meant to him, the roll and flip of data on a screen. He studied the figural diagrams that brought organic patterns into play, birdwing and chambered shell. It was shallow thinking to maintain that numbers and charts were the cold compression of unruly human energies, every sort of yearning and midnight sweat reduced to lucid units in the financial markets. In fact data itself was soulful and glowing, a dynamic aspect of the life process. This was the eloquence of alphabets and numeric systems, now fully realized in electronic form, in the zero-oneness of the world, the digital imperative that defined every breath of the planet's living billions. Here was the heave of the biosphere. Our bodies and oceans were here, knowable and whole.

The car began to move. He saw the first of the haircutting salons to his right, on the northwest corner, Filles et Garçons. He sensed Torval waiting, up front, for the order to stop the car.

He glimpsed the marquee of the second establishment, not far ahead, and spoke a coded phrase to a signal processor in the partition, the slide between the driver and rear cabin. This generated a command on one of the dashboard screens.

The car came to a stop in front of the apartment building that was situated between the two salons. He got out and went into the tunneled passage, not waiting for the doorman to shuffle to his phone. He entered the enclosed space of the courtyard, mentally naming what was in it, the shade-happy euonymus and lobelia, the dark-star coleus, the honey locust with its pinnate leaves and unsplit pods. He could not quite summon the Latin name of the tree but knew it would come to him within the hour or somewhere deep in the running lull of the next sleepless night.

He walked under a cross-vaulted arch of white latticework planted with climbing hydrangeas and then stepped into the building proper.

A minute later he was in her apartment.

She put a hand to his chest, self-dramatically, to determine he was here and real. Then they began to stumble and clutch, working toward the bedroom. They hit the doorpost and bounced. One of her shoes began to angle off but she could not shake free and he had to kick it away. He pressed her against the wall drawing, a minimalist grid executed over several weeks by two of the artist's adjutants working with measuring instruments and graphite pencils.

They did not get serious about undressing until they were finished making love.

"Was I expecting you?"

"Just passing by."

They stood on opposite sides of the bed, bending and flexing to remove final items of clothing.

"Thought you'd drop in, did you? That's nice. I'm glad. Been a while. I read about it, of course."

She lay prone now, head turned on the pillow, and watched him.

"Or did I see it on TV?"

"What?"

"What? The wedding. How strange you didn't tell me."

"Not so strange."

"Not so strange. Two great fortunes," she said. "Like one of the great arranged marriages of old empire Europe."

"Except I'm a world citizen with a New York pair of balls."

Hoisting his genitals in his hand. Then he lay on the bed on his back staring into a painted paper lamp suspended from the ceiling.

"How many billions together do you two represent?"

"She's a poet."

"Is that what she is? I thought she was a Shifrin."

"A little of both."

"So rich and crisp. Does she let you touch her personal parts?"

"You look gorgeous today."

"For someone who's forty-seven and finally understands what her problem is."

"What's that?"

"Life is too contemporary. How old is your consort? Never mind. I don't want to know. Tell me to shut up. One more question first. Is she good in bed?"

"I don't know yet."

"That's the trouble with old money," she said. "Now tell me to shut up."

He placed a hand on her buttock. They lay a while in silence. She was a scorched blonde named Didi Fancher.

"I know something you want to know."

He said, "What?"

"There's a Rothko in private hands that I have privileged knowledge of. It is about to become available."

"You've seen it."

"Three or four years ago. Yes. And it is luminous."

He said, "What about the chapel?"

"What about it?"

"I've been thinking about the chapel."

"You can't buy the goddamn chapel."

"How do you know? Contact the principals."

"I thought you'd be thrilled about the painting. One painting. You don't have an important Rothko. You've always wanted one. We've talked about this."

"How many paintings in his chapel?"

"I don't know. Fourteen, fifteen."

"If they sell me the chapel, I'll keep it intact. Tell them."

"Keep it intact where?"

"In my apartment. There's sufficient space. I can make more space."

"But people need to see it."

"Let them buy it. Let them outbid me."

"Forgive the pissy way I say this. But the Rothko Chapel belongs to the world."

"It's mine if I buy it."

She reached back and slapped his hand off her ass.

He said, "How much do they want for it?"

"They don't want to sell the chapel. And I don't want to give you lessons in self-denial and social responsibility. Because I don't believe for a minute you're as crude as you sound."

"You'd believe it. You'd accept the way I think and act if I came from another culture. If I were a pygmy dictator," he said, "or a cocaine warlord. Someone from the fanatical tropics. You'd love it, wouldn't you? You'd cherish the excess, the monomania. Such people cause a delicious stir in other people. People such as you. But there has to be a separation. If they look and smell like you, it gets confusing."

He pushed his armpit toward her face.

"Here lies Didi. Trapped in all the old puritanisms."

He rolled belly down and they lay close, hips and shoulders touching. He licked along the rim of her ear and put his face in her hair, rooting softly.

He said, "How much?"

"What does it mean to spend money? A dollar. A million."

"For a painting?"

"For anything."

"I have two private elevators now. One is programmed

28

to play Satie's piano pieces and to move at one-quarter normal speed. This is right for Satie and this is the elevator I take when I'm in a certain, let's say, unsettled mood. Calms me, makes me whole."

"Who's the other elevator?"

"Brutha Fez."

"Who's that?"

"The Sufi rap star. You don't know this?"

"I miss things."

"Cost me major money and made me an enemy of the people, requisitioning that second elevator."

"Money for paintings. Money for anything. I had to learn how to understand money," she said. "I grew up comfortably. Took me a while to think about money and actually look at it. I began to look at it. Look closely at bills and coins. I learned how it felt to make money and spend it. It felt intensely satisfying. It helped me be a person. But I don't know what money is anymore."

"I'm losing money by the ton today. Many millions. Betting against the yen."

"Isn't the yen asleep?"

"Currency markets never close. And the Nikkei runs all day and night now. All the major exchanges. Seven days a week."

"I missed that. I miss a lot. How many millions?"

"Hundreds of millions."

She thought about that. She began to whisper now.

"How old are you? Twenty-eight?"

"Twenty-eight," he said.

"I think you want this Rothko. Pricey. But yes. You totally need to have it."

"Why?"

"It will remind you that you're alive. You have something in you that's receptive to the mysteries."

He laid his middle finger lightly in the rut between her buttocks.

He said, "The mysteries."

"Don't you see yourself in every picture you love? You feel a radiance wash through you. It's something you can't analyze or speak about clearly. What are you doing at that moment? You're looking at a picture on a wall. That's all. But it makes you feel alive in the world. It tells you yes, you're here. And yes, you have a range of being that's deeper and sweeter than you knew."

He made a fist and wedged it between her thighs, turning it slowly back and forth.

"I want you to go to the chapel and make an offer. Whatever it takes. I want everything that's there. Walls and all.'

She didn't move for a moment. Then she disengaged, the body easing free of the goading hand.

He watched her getting dressed. She dressed in a summary manner, appearing to think ahead to some business that needed completing, whatever he'd interrupted on his arrival. She was in post-sensual time, fitting an arm to a creamy sleeve, and looked drabber and sadder now. He wanted a reason to despise her.

"I remember what you told me once."

30

"What's that?"

"Talent is more erotic when it's wasted."

"What did I mean?" she said.

"You meant I was ruthlessly efficient. Talented, yes. In business, in personal acquisitions. Organizing my life in general."

"Did I mean lovemaking as well?"

"I don't know. Did you?"

"Not quite ruthless. But yes. Talented. And a commanding presence as well. Dressed or undressed. Another talent, I suppose."

"But there was something missing for you. Or nothing missing. That was the point," he said. "All this talent and drive. Utilized. Consistently put to good use."

She was looking for a lost shoe.

"But that's not true anymore," she said.

He watched her. He didn't think he wanted to be surprised, even by a woman, this woman, who'd taught him how to look, how to feel enchantment damp on his face, the melt of pleasure inside a brushstroke or band of color.

She dipped toward the bed. But before she plucked her shoe from under a quilt that had spilled to the floor, she engaged him at eye level.

"Not since an element of doubt began to enter your life."

"Doubt? What is doubt?" He said, "There is no doubt. Nobody doubts anymore."

She stepped into the shoe and adjusted her skirt.

"You're beginning to think it's more interesting to doubt than to act. It takes more courage to doubt."

She was whispering, still, and turned away from him now.

"If this makes me sexier, then where are you going?"

She was going to answer the telephone that was ringing in the study.

He had one sock on when it came to him. *G. triacanthos*. He knew it would come to him and it did. The botanical name of the tree in the courtyard. *Gleditsia triacanthos*. The honey locust.

He felt better now. He knew who he was and reached for his shirt, dressing in double time.

Torval was standing outside the door. Their eyes did not meet. They went to the elevator and rode to the lobby in silence. He let Torval exit first and check the area. He had to concede that the man did this well, in a soft choreography of tacking moves, disciplined and clean. Then they walked through the courtyard and out to the street.

They stood by the car. Torval indicated the haircut that waited in either direction, only yards away. Then his eyes went cool and still. He was hearing a voice in his ear bud. There was a pitch to the moment, a sense of intent expectation.

"Threat condition blue," he said finally. "Man down."

The driver held open the door. Eric did not look at the driver. There were times when he thought he might look at the driver. But he had not done this yet.

32

The man down was Arthur Rapp, managing director of the International Monetary Fund. Arthur Rapp had just been assassinated in Nike North Korea. Happened only a minute ago. Eric watched it happen again, in obsessive replays, as the car crawled toward a choke point on Lexington Avenue. He hated Arthur Rapp. He'd hated him before he met him. It was a hatred with the purest bloodlines, orderly, based on differences of theory and interpretation. Then he met the man and hated him personally and chaotically, with sizable violence of heart.

He was killed live on the Money Channel. It was past midnight in Pyongyang and he was making final comments to an interviewer for the benefit of North American audiences after a historic day and night of ceremonies, receptions, dinners, speeches and toasts.

Eric watched him sign a document on one screen and prepare to die on another.

A man in a short-sleeve shirt came into camera range and began to stab Arthur Rapp in the face and neck. Arthur Rapp clutched the man and seemed to draw him nearer as if to share a confidence. They tumbled together to the floor, tangled in the mike cord of the interviewer. She was dragged down with them, a willowy woman whose slit skirt ran up her thigh and became the pivotal point of observation.

Horns were blowing in the street.

There was a close-up on one of the screens. It was Arthur Rapp's pulpy face blowing outward in spasms of shock and pain. It resembled a mass of pressed vegetable matter. Eric wanted them to show it again. *Show it again.* They did this, of course, and he knew they would do it repeatedly into the night, our night, until the sensation drained out of it or everyone in the world had seen it, whichever came first, but he could see it again if he wished, any time, through scan retrieval, a technology that seemed already oppressively sluggish, or he could recover a slow-motion shot of the willowy woman and her hand mike being sucked into the terror and he could sit here for hours wanting to fuck her then and there in the bloodwhirl of knife and random limbs and slashed carotids, amid the staccato cries of the flailing assassin, cell phone clipped to his belt, and the gaseous bloated moans of the dying Arthur Rapp.

A tour bus blocked the route across the avenue. It was a double decker with smoke rolling from its underbelly and rows of woeful heads poking from the top tier, unstirring Swedes and Chinese, their fanny packs stuffed with currency.

Michael Chin was still in the jump seat, facing rearward. He'd listened to the audio account of the assassination but had not turned to look at the screens.

Eric watched him now, wondering whether the young man's restraint was a form of moral rigor or an apathy so deep it was not pierced by the muses, even, of sex and death.

"While you were away," Chin said.

"Yes. Tell me."

"There was a report that consumer spending is weakening in Japan." He spoke in a newscaster's voice. "Raising doubts about the country's economic strength."

"See. What. I said as much."

"The yen is expected to fade. The yen will sink a bit."

"There we are. See. Has to happen. The situation has to change. The yen can't go any higher."

Torval came walking back to this end of the car. Eric lowered the window. Windows still had to be lowered.

Torval said, "A word."

"Yes."

"The complex recommends extra security."

"You're not happy about this."

"First a threat to the president."

"You're confident you can handle whatever comes up."

"Now this attack on the managing director."

"Accept their recommendation."

He raised the window. How did he feel about additional security? He felt refreshed. The death of Arthur Rapp was refreshing. The prospective dip in the yen was invigorating.

He scanned the visual display units. They were deployed at graded distances from the rear seat, flat plasma screens of assorted sizes, some in a cluster framework, a few others projected singly from side cabinets. The grouping was a work of video sculpture, handsome and airy, with protean potential, each unit designed to swing out, fold up or operate independent of the others.

He liked the volume low or the sound turned off.

They were climbing down out of the tour bus now. It seemed to be sinking into the dark smoke that foamed up around it. A derelict tried to board, dressed in bubble wrap. There were sirens in the distance, fire trucks caught in traffic, the sound hanging in the air, undopplered, and car horns blowing locally, another hardness upon the day.

He felt his elation deepen. He slid open the sunroof and thrust his head into the reeling scene. The bank towers loomed just beyond the avenue. They were covert structures for all their size, hard to see, so common and monotonic, tall, sheer, abstract, with standard setbacks, and block-long, and interchangeable, and he had to concentrate to see them.

They looked empty from here. He liked that idea. They were made to be the last tall things, made empty, designed to hasten the future. They were the end of the outside world. They weren't here, exactly. They were in the future, a time beyond geography and touchable money and the people who stack and count it.

He sat down and looked at Chin, who was biting the dead skin at the side of his thumbnail. He watched him gnaw. This was not another of Michael's tender reveries. He was gnawing, grinding his teeth on the hangnail, then the nail itself, the base of the nail, the pale arc of quarter moon, the lunula, and there was something awful and atavistic in the scene, Chin unborn, curled in a membranous sac, a scary little geek-headed humanoid, sucking his scalloped hands.

Why is a hangnail called a hangnail? It's an alteration of agnail, which is Middle English, Eric happened to know, from Old English, with roots in torment and pain.

Chin loosed one of his vegetarian farts. Mode control ate it at once. Then there was an opening and the car bucked and lurched, veering in a screech around the tour bus and across the avenue. The man at the taco cart solemnly watched. The car wobbled over the curbstone and sphinctered free and Chin's eyes came out of lunar seclusion when it raced all the way to Park along a surreal length of empty street.

"Time for you to do what."

"Yes. All right," Chin said.

"You don't know this? We both know this."

"There's work to do at the office. Yes. I need to retrace events over time and see what I can find that applies."

"Nothing applies. But it's there. It charts. You'll see it."

"I need to back-test currencies, I don't know, like into the misty dawn."

"We can't wait for the misty dawn."

"Then I'll do it here. To save time. That should make you happy. I do time cycles in my sleep. Years, months, weeks. All the subtle patterns I've found. All the mathematics I've brought to time cycles and price histories. Then you start finding hourly cycles. Then stinking minutes. Then down to seconds."

"You see this in fruit flies and heart attacks. Common forces at work."

"I'm so obsolete I don't have to chew my food."

"You can't stay here."

"I like it here."

"No, you don't."

"I like riding backwards." Chin spoke in his newscaster voice. "He died as he lived. Backwards. Details after the game."

He felt good. He felt stronger than he had in days, or weeks maybe, or longer. The light was red. He saw Jane Melman on the other side of the avenue, his chief of finance, dressed in jogging shorts and a tank top, moving in a wolverine lope. She stopped at the prearranged pickup spot, next to the bronze statue of a man hailing a cab. Then she looked in Eric's direction, squinting, trying to determine whether the limousine was his or someone else's. He knew what she would say to him, first line, word for word, and he looked forward to hearing it. He could hear it already in the nasal airstream of her vernacular. He liked knowing what was coming. It confirmed the presence of some hereditary script available to those who could decode it.

Chin hopped out the door before the car crossed Park Avenue. There was a woman in gray spandex on the median strip holding a dead rat aloft. A performance piece, it seemed. The light went green and horns began to blow. On buildings everywhere in the area the names of financial institutions were engraved on bronze markers, carved in marble, etched in gold leaf on beveled glass.

Melman was running in place. When the car stopped at

the corner, she left the shadow of the glass tower behind her and came bumping through the rear door, all elbows and gleaming knees, a web phone pouched on her belly. She was breathless and sweaty from her run and fell into the jump seat with the kind of grim deliverance that marks a deadweight drop to the toilet.

"All these limos, my god, that you can't tell one from another."

He narrowed his eyes and nodded.

"We could be kids on prom night," she said, "or some dumb wedding wherever. What's the charm of identical?"

He glanced out the window, speaking softly, so cool to the subject that he had to deliver his remark to the steel and glass out there, the indifferent street.

"That I'm a powerful person who chooses not to demarcate his territory with singular driblets of piss is what? Is something I need to apologize for?"

"I want to go home and tongue-kiss my Maxima."

The car was not moving. There was a noise beating down that made people cover up when they walked past, rumbling gutturals from the granite tower being raised on the south side of the street, named for a huge investment firm.

"You know what today is, incidentally."

"I know."

"It's my day off, damn it."

"I know this."

"I need this extra day desperately."

"I know this."

"You don't know this. You can't know what it's like. I am a single struggling mother."

"We have a situation here."

"I am a mother running in the park when my phone explodes in my navel. I think it's the kids' nanny, who never calls until the fever reaches a hundred and five. But it's the situation. We have a situation all right. We have a yen carry that could crush us in hours."

"Take some water. Sit on the banquette."

"I like face-to-face. And I don't need to look at all those screens," she said. "I know what's happening."

"The yen will fall."

"That's right."

"Consumer spending's down," he said.

"That's right. Besides which the Bank of Japan left interest rates unchanged."

"This happened today?"

"This happened tonight. In Tokyo. I called a source at the Nikkei."

"While running."

"While flinging my body down Madison Avenue to get here on time."

"The yen can't go any higher."

"That's true. That's right," she said. "Except it just did."

He looked at her, pink and dripping. The car moved faintly forward now and he felt the stir of a melancholy that seemed to cross deep vales of space to reach him here in the midtown grid. He looked out the window, seeing

40

them in odd composite, people on the street, and they waved at taxis and crossed against the light, all and one together, and stood in line at cash machines in the Chase Bank.

She told him he looked mopish.

Buses rumbled up the avenue in pairs, hacking and panting, buses abreast or single file, sending people to the sidewalk in sprints, live prey, nothing new, and that's where construction workers were eating lunch, seated against bank walls, legs stretched, rusty boots, appraising eyes, all trained on the streaming people, the march-past, checking looks and pace and style, women in brisk skirts, half running, sandaled women wearing headsets, women in floppy shorts, tourists, others high and slick with fingernails from vampire movies, long, fanged and frescoed, and the workers were alert for freakishness of any kind, people whose hair or clothing or manner of stride mock what the workers do, forty stories up, or schmucks with cell phones, who rankled them in general.

These were scenes that normally roused him, the great rapacious flow, where the physical will of the city, the ego fevers, the assertions of industry, commerce and crowds shape every anecdotal moment.

He heard himself speak from some middle distance.

"I didn't sleep last night," he said.

The car crossed Madison and stopped in front of the Mercantile Library as planned. There were eating places up and down the street. He thought of people eating, lives running out over lunch. What was behind such a thought? He thought of bussers combing crumbs off the tables. The waiters and bussers did not die. It was only the patrons who failed to show up, one by one, over time, for soup with packaged crackers on the side.

A man in a suit and tie approached the car, carrying a small satchel. Eric looked away. His mind went blank except for some business concerning the pathos of the word satchel. It is possible for the mind to go blank in a tactic of evasion or suppression, the reaction to a menace so impending, a tailored man with a suitcase bomb, that there is no blessing to be found in the most resourceful thought, no time for an eddy of sensation, the natural rush that might accompany danger.

When the man tapped on the window, Eric did not look at him.

Then Torval was there, tight-eyed, a hand in his jacket, with two of his aides angling in, male and female, becomingly strikingly lifelike as they emerged from the visual static of the lunch swarm in the street.

Torval leaned into the man.

He said, "Who the fuck are you?"

"Excuse me."

"There's a time limit."

"Dr. Ingram."

Torval had the man's arm yanked up behind him now. He pressed the man into the side of the automobile. Eric leaned toward the window and lowered it. Food odors mingled in the air, coriander and onion soup, the funk of beef patties frying. The aides formed a loose cordon, both facing outward from the action.

Two women came out of Yodo of Japan, then went back in.

Eric looked at the man. He wanted Torval to shoot him or put the weapon at least to his head.

He said, "Who the fuck are you?"

"Dr. Ingram."

"Where is Dr. Nevius?"

"Called away suddenly. Personal matter."

"Speak slowly and clearly."

"Called away suddenly. I don't know. Family crisis. I'm the associate."

Eric thought about this.

"I flushed out your ear holes once."

Eric looked at Torval and nodded briefly.

Then he raised the window.

He sat stripped to the waist. Ingram opened the satchel to a set of vivid instruments. He put the stethoscope to Eric's chest. He realized, Eric did, why his undershirt was missing. He'd left it on the floor of Didi Fancher's bedroom.

He looked past Ingram while the doctor listened to his heart valves open and close. The car moved incrementally westward. He didn't know why stethoscopes were still in use. They were lost tools of antiquity, quaint as blood-sucking worms.

Jane Melman said, "You do this what."

"What. Every day."

"No matter."

"Wherever I am. That's right. No matter."

She tipped back her head and plunged a bottle of spring water into the middle of her face.

Ingram did an echocardiogram. Eric was on his back, with a skewed view of the monitor, and wasn't sure whether he was watching a computerized mapping of his heart or a picture of the thing itself. It throbbed forcefully on-screen. The image was only a foot away but the heart assumed another context, one of distance and immensity, beating in the blood plum raptures of a galaxy in formation. What mystery he glimpsed in this functional muscle. He felt the passion of the body, its adaptive drive over geologic time, the poetry and chemistry of its origins in the dust of old exploding stars. How dwarfed he felt by his own heart. There it was and it awed him, to see his life beneath his breastbone in image-forming units, hammering on outside him.

He said nothing to Ingram. He didn't want to talk to the associate. He talked to Nevius now and then. Nevius had definition. He was white-haired, tall and stalwart, with a trace of Middle Europe in his voice. Ingram spoke in mutters of instruction. Breathe deep. Turn left. It was hard for him to say something he hadn't already said, words arranged in the same tedious sequence, a thousand times before.

Melman said, "So you do what. Same routine every day."

44

"Varies, depending."

"So he comes to your house, nice, on weekends."

"We die, Jane, on weekends. People. It happens."

"You're right. I didn't think of that."

"We die because it's the weekend."

He was still on his back. She sat facing the top of his head, speaking to a point slightly above it.

"I thought we were moving. But we're not anymore."

"The president's in town."

"You're right. I forgot. I thought I saw him when I ran out of the park. There was an entourage of limousines going down Fifth, with a motorcycle escort. I thought all these limos for the president I can understand. But it was somebody famous's funeral."

"We die every day," he told her.

He sat on the table now and Ingram looked for swollen lymph nodes under his arms. Eric pointed out a plug of sebum and cell debris on his lower abdomen, a blackhead, slightly sinister.

"What do we do about this?"

"Let it express itself."

"What. Do nothing."

"Let it express itself," Ingram said.

Eric liked the sound of that. It was not unevocative. He tried to notice the associate. He had a mustache, for example. Eric hadn't seen it until now. He expected to see glasses as well. But the man did not wear glasses although he seemed to be someone who should, based on facial typology and general demeanor, a man who'd worn glasses since early boyhood, looking overprotected and marginalized, persecuted by the other kids. He was a man you'd swear wore glasses.

He asked Eric to stand. He adjusted the examining table to half length. Then he asked him to drop his pants and shorts and to bend over the near end of the table, legs apart.

He did this and was facing his chief of finance.

She said, "So look. We have two rumors working in our favor. First there's bankruptcies for six straight months. More each month. More on the way. Large Japanese corporations. This is good."

"The yen has to drop."

"This is loss of faith. It will force the yen to drop."

"The dollar will settle up."

"The yen will drop," she said.

He heard a slidy rustle of latex. Then the Ingram finger entered.

"Where is Chin?" she said.

"Working on visual patterns."

"This thing doesn't chart."

"It charts."

"It doesn't chart the way you chart technology stocks. You can find real patterns there. Locate predictable components. This is different."

"We are teaching him to see."

"You should do the seeing. You're the seer. What is he? A kid. He has the streak in the hair. He has the earring."

"He doesn't have the earring."

"If he was any more dreamy, we'd have to put him on life support."

He said, "What's the second rumor?"

Ingram examined the prostate for signs. He palpated, the finger slyly prodding the surface of the gland through the rectal wall. There was pain, probably just muscles tensing in the anal canal. But it hurt. It was pain. It traveled the circuitry of nerve cells. From his stooped position, Eric looked directly into Jane's face. He liked doing this, which surprised him. In the office she was an edgy presence, skeptical, adversarial, aloof, with a gift for sustained complaint. Here, she was a single running mother in a foldout seat, knock-kneed and touchingly, somehow, gaunt. A splash of hair lay moist and flat on her forehead, showing the first faint veining of gray. The water bottle dangled from a lank hand.

She did not recede from his gaze. She made complete eye contact. Her clavicle showed knobby above the droop of her tank top. He wanted to lick the sweat off the inside of her wrist. She was wrists and shinbones and unbalmed lips.

"There's a rumor it seems involving the finance minister. He's supposed to resign any time now," she said. "Some kind of scandal about a misconstrued comment. He made a comment about the economy that may have been misconstrued. The whole country is analyzing the grammar and syntax of this comment. Or it wasn't even

47

what he said. It was when he paused. They are trying to construe the meaning of the pause. It could be deeper, even, than grammar. It could be breathing."

When Nevius did the finger, it was in and out in seconds. Ingram was probing for some murky fact. Jane was the fact. She had the bottle in her crotch, knees flopped outward now, and watched him. Her mouth was open, showing large gapped teeth. Something passed between them, deeply, a sympathy beyond the standard meanings that also encompassed these meanings, pity, affinity, tenderness, the whole physiology of neural maneuver, of heartbeat and secretion, some vast sexus of arousal drawing him toward her, complicatedly, with Ingram's finger up his ass.

"So the whole economy convulses," she said, "because the man took a breath."

He felt these things. He felt the pain. It traveled the pathways. It informed the ganglion and spinal cord. He was here in his body, the structure he wanted to dismiss in theory even when he was shaping it under the measured effect of barbells and weights. He wanted to judge it redundant and transferable. It was convertible to wave arrays of information. It was the thing he watched on the oval screen when he wasn't watching Jane.

"You grip the water bottle."

"It's that soft type plastic."

"You grip it. You choke it."

"It's a matter-of-fact thing."

"It's sexual tension."

48

"It's everyday nervousness in a life."

"It's sexual tension," he said.

He told Ingram to reach over with his free hand and fish the sunglasses out of the suit jacket on the hanger nearby. The associate managed to do this. Eric put on the glasses.

"Days like this."

"What?" she said.

"My mood shifts and bends. But when I'm alive and heightened, I'm super-acute. Do you know what I see when I look at you? I see a woman who wants to live shamelessly in her body. Tell me this is not the truth. You want to follow your body into idleness and fleshiness. That's why you have to run, to escape the drift of your basic nature. Tell me I'm making it up. You can't do that. It's there in your face, all of it, the way it rarely shows in any face. What do I see? Something lazy, sexy and insatiable."

"I'm comfortable with that."

"This is the woman you are inside the life. Looking at you, what? I'm more excited than I've been since the first burning nights of adolescent frenzy. Excited and confused. I look at you and feel an erection stirring even as the situation argues strenuously against it."

"It can't afford to be hard. It won't allow itself psychologically," she said. "It knows what's going on back there."

"All the same. Days like this. I look at you and feel electric. Tell me you don't feel it too. The minute you sat there in that whole tragic regalia of running. That whole sad business of Judeo-Christian jogging. You were not born to run. I look at you. I know what you are. You are sloppy-bodied, smelly and wet. A woman who was born to sit strapped in a chair while a man tells her how much she excites him."

"How come we've never spent this kind of time together?"

"Sex finds us out. Sex sees through us. That's why it's so shattering. It strips us of appearances. I see a near naked woman in her exhaustion and need, stroking a plastic bottle pressed between her thighs. Am I honor-bound to think of her as an executive and a mother? She sees a man in a posture of rank humiliation. Is that who I think he is, pants around his ankles and butt flung back? What are the questions he asks himself from this position in the world? Large questions maybe. Questions such as science obsessively asks. *Why something and not nothing? Why music and not noise?* Beautiful questions strangely suited to his low moment. Or is he limited in perspective, thinking only about the moment itself? Thinking about the pain."

The pain was local but seemed to absorb everything around it, organs, objects, street sounds, words. It was a point of hellish perception that was steady-state, unchanging in degree, and not a point at all but some bundled other brain, a counter-consciousness, but not that either, located at the base of his bladder. He operated from within. He could think and speak of other things but only within the pain. He was living in the gland, in the scalding fact of his biology.

"Does he regret surrendering his dignity and pride? Or

is there a secret wish for self-abasement?" He smiled at Jane. "Is his manhood a sham? Does he love himself or hate himself? I don't think he knows. Or it changes minute to minute. Or the question is so implicit in everything he does that he can't get outside it to answer."

He thought he was serious. He did not think he was speaking for effect. These were serious questions. He knew they were serious but was not sure.

"Days like this. He snaps a finger and a flame shoots up. Every sensitivity, all his attunements. Things are ready to happen that normally never do. She knows what he means, that they don't even have to touch. The same thing that's happening to him is happening to her. She doesn't need to crawl under the table and suck his dick. Too trite to interest either one of them. The flow is strong between them. The emotional tone. Let it express itself. He sees her in her wallow and feels his pelvic muscles begin to quiver. He says, Tell me to stop and I'll stop. But he doesn't wait for her to reply. There isn't time. The tails of his sperm cells are lashing already. She is his sweetheart and lover and slut undying. He doesn't have to do the unspeakable thing he wants to do. He only has to speak it. Because they're beyond every model of established behavior. He only has to say the words."

"Say the words."

"I want to bottle-fuck you slowly with my sunglasses on."

Her feet flew out from under her. She uttered a thing, a sound, herself, her soul in rapid rising inflection.

He saw his face on the screen, eyes closed, mouth framed in a soundless little simian howl.

He knew the spycam operated in real time, or was supposed to. How could he see himself if his eyes were closed? There wasn't time to analyze. He felt his body catching up to the independent image.

Then man and woman reached completion more or less together, touching neither each other nor themselves.

The associate tore the glove off his hand and slapped it in the waste bin, the rip and the discard, dark with meaning.

Horns were blowing up and down the street. Eric began to dress, waiting for Ingram to use the word asymmetrical. But he said nothing. His real doctor, Nevius, had used the word once, in palpation, without elaborating. He saw Nevius nearly every day but had never asked what the word implied.

He liked to track answers to hard questions. This was his method, to attain mastery over ideas and people. But there was something about the idea of asymmetry. It was intriguing in the world outside the body, a counterforce to balance and calm, the riddling little twist, subatomic, that made creation happen. There was the serpentine word itself, slightly off kilter, with the single additional letter that changes everything. But when he removed the word from its cosmological register and applied it to the body of a male mammal, his body, he began to feel pale and spooked. He felt a certain perverse reverence toward the word. A fear of, a distance from. When he heard the word spoken in a context of urine and semen and when he thought of the word in the shadow of pissed pants, one, and limp-dick desolation, two, he was haunted to the point of superstitious silence.

He took off his sunglasses and looked closely at Ingram. He tried to read his face. It was empty of affect. He thought of putting his sunglasses on the associate's face, to make him real, give him meaning in the sweep of other people's perceptions, but the glasses would have to be clear and thick-lensed and life-defining. If you knew the man ten years, it might take you all that time to notice he did not wear glasses. It was a face that was lost without them.

It was not Ingram who spoke. It was Jane Melman, pausing at the open door before she resumed her interrupted run.

"I want to say something that is deeply uncomplicated. There is time to choose. You can ease off and take a loss and come back stronger. It is not too late. You can make this choice. You've done great work for our investors in strong and choppy markets both. Most asset managers underperform the market. You've outperformed it, consistently, and you've never been influenced by the sweep of the crowd. This is one of your gifts."

He was not listening. He was looking past her to a figure at the cash machine outside the Israeli bank on the northeast corner, a slight man mumbling in his teeth.

"We've profited, we've flourished even as other funds have stumbled," she said. "Yes, the yen will fall. I don't think the yen can go any higher. But in the meantime you have to draw back. Pull back. I am advising you in this matter not only as your chief of finance but as a woman who would still be married to her husbands if they had looked at her the way you have looked at me here today."

He was not looking at her now. She shut the door and began running north on Fifth Avenue, past the shabby man at the ATM. There was something familiar about him. It wasn't his khaki field jacket or paper-shredded hair. Maybe it was his slouch. But Eric didn't care whether this was someone he'd once known. There were many people he'd once known. Some were dead, others in forced retirement, spending quiet time alone in their toilets or walking in the woods with their three-legged dogs.

He was thinking about automated teller machines. The term was aged and burdened by its own historical memory. It worked at cross-purposes, unable to escape the inference of fuddled human personnel and jerky moving parts. The term was part of the process that the device was meant to replace. It was anti-futuristic, so cumbrous and mechanical that even the acronym seemed dated.

Ingram folded the examining table back into the cabinet. He packed his satchel and went out the door, turning briefly to look at Eric. He was stationary, only a couple of feet away, but already lost in the crowd, forgotten even as he spoke, wide-eyed, with studied detachment in his voice.

"Your prostate is asymmetrical," he said.

The Confessions
of Benno Levin

NIGHT

He is dead, word for word. I turned him over and looked at
him. His eyes were mercifully closed. But what does mercy
have to do with it? There was a brief sound in his throat
that I could spend weeks trying to describe. But how can
you make words out of sounds? These are two separate systems that we miserably try to link.

This resembles something he would say. I must be
mouthing his words again. Because I'm sure he said it
once, walking past my workstation to the person who was
with him, in reference to such and such. Mirrors and
images. Or sex and love. These are two separate systems
that we miserably try to link.

Allow me to speak for myself. I had a job and a family.
I struggled to love and provide. How many of you know
the true and bitter force of that simple word provide? They
always said I was erratic. He is erratic. He has problems of

personality and hygiene. He walks, whatever, funny. I never heard a single one of these statements but knew they were being made the way you sense something in a person's look that does not have to be spoken.

I made a phone threat that I didn't believe. They took the threat to be credible, which I knew they had to do, considering my knowledge of the firm and the personnel. But I didn't know how to track him down. He moved about the city without pattern. He had armed escorts. The building where he lived was unapproachable in my current state of randomized attire. And I accepted this. Even at the firm, it was not easy to find his office. It changed all the time. Or he voided it to work elsewhere, or work wherever he happened to be, or work at home in the annex because he did not really separate live and work, or to travel and think, or to spend time reading in his rumored lake house in the mountains.

My obsessions are mind things, not geared to action.

Now I'm in a position where I can talk to his corpse. I can speak without interruptions or corrections. He can't tell me this or that is the case or I am shaming myself or fooling myself. Not thinking straight. This is the crime he placed in the hall of fame of horrors.

When I try to suppress my anger, I suffer spells of *hwa-byung* (Korea). This is cultural panic mainly, which I caught on the Internet.

I was assistant professor of computer applications. Maybe I said this already, in a community college. Then I left to make my million.

56

The pencil I'm writing with is yellow, with the numeral 2. I want to note the tools I'm using, just for the record.

I was always aware of what they said in words or looks. It is what people think they see in another person that makes his reality. If they think he walks at a slant, then he walks at a slant, uncoordinated, because this is his role in the lives around him, and if they say his clothes don't fit, he will learn to be neglectful of his wardrobe as a means of scorning them and inflicting punishment on himself.

I make mind speeches all the time. So do you, only not always. I do it all the time, long speeches to someone I can never identify. But I'm beginning to think it's him.

I have my paper, legal size, white with blue lines. I want to write ten thousand pages. But already I see that I'm repeating myself. I'm repeating myself.

After I turned him over I went through his pockets and found nothing. One of his pockets was torn. He had a crusty purple wound on his head, not that I am interested in description. I am interested in money. I was looking for money. He had one half a haircut but not the other and wore shoes but no socks. The body smell was foul.

I steal electricity from a lamppost. I doubt if this occurred to him, for my living space.

I've suffered many reversals but I'm not one of those scanted men you see in the street, living and thinking in minutes. I live at the ends of the earth philosophically. I collect things, it is true, from local sidewalks. What people discard could make a nation. Sometimes I hear my voice when I am speaking. I am speaking to someone and hear the sound of my voice, third person, filling the air around my head.

The windows were sealed by the City when they condemned the building. But I pried one board loose to let in air. I don't live an unreal life. I live a practical life of starting over, with middle-class values intact. I'm knocking down walls because I don't want to live in a set of little quads where other people lived, doors and narrow hallways, whole families with their packed lives and so many steps to the bed and so many steps to the door. I want to live an open life of the mind where my Confessions can thrive.

But there are times when I want to rub myself against a door or wall, for the sympathetic contact.

I wanted his pocket money for its personal qualities, not its value so much. I wanted its intimacy and touch, his touch, the stain of his personal dirt. I wanted to rub the bills over my face to remind me why I shot him.

For a while I could not stop looking at the body. I looked inside his mouth for signs of rot. That's when I heard the sound in his throat. I thought in all expectancy he was going to talk to me. I wouldn't mind talking to him some more. After all we'd said in the long night I realize there's more for me to say. There are great themes running through my mind. The themes of loneliness and human discard. The theme of who do I hate when there's no one left.

The complex is the intelligence unit of the firm. This is who I called with my mostly empty threat. I knew they would interpret my comments as the specialized knowledge of a former employee and would gather rapid data on such. It was satisfying to me, telling them their own names, even somebody's mother's maiden name in a brilliant and telling thrust, and detailing the procedures and routines. I was in their heads now, making contact. I didn't have to carry the burden alone.

I have my writing desk, which I dragged along the sidewalk, through the alley and up the stairs. This was an undertaking of days, with a system of wedges and ropes. This was two days I needed to do this.

I never felt a distinction over time between child and man, boy and man. I was never consciously a child as the term is usually applied. I feel like the same thing I always was.

I used to write him letters after they let me go but stopped because I knew it was pathetic. I also knew there was something in my life that needed to be pathetic but I forced myself to break off contact. The fact that he would never see the letters was not an issue. I would see them. The issue was writing them and seeing them myself. So think how surprised I was that I did not have to track him and stalk him, which I was unfitted to do and anyway haunted by opposing forces concerning does he die or not.

And whatever I said to them on the phone and however rapidly they gathered data, how could they trace me to where and how I live?

I don't own a watch or clock. I think of time in other totalities now. I think of my personal time-span set against the vast numerations, the time of the earth, the stars, the incoherent light-years, the age of the universe, etc.

World is supposed to mean something that's self-contained. But nothing is self-contained. Everything enters something else. My small days spill into light-years. This is why I can only pretend to be someone. And this is why I felt derived at first, working on these pages. I didn't know if it was me that was writing so much as someone I want to sound like.

I still have my bank that I visit systematically to look at the last literal dollars remaining in my account. I do this for the ongoing psychology of it, to know I have money in an institution. And because cash machines have a charisma that still speaks to me.

I am working on this journal while a man lies dead ten feet away. I wonder about this. Twelve feet away. They said I had problems of normalcy and they demoted me to lesser currencies. I became a minor technical element in the firm, a technical fact. I was generic labor to them. And I accepted this. Then they let me go without notice or severance package. And I accepted this.

One of my syndromes is agitated behavior and extreme confusion. This is known in Haiti and East Africa as delirious gusts in translation. In the world today everything is shared. What kind of misery is it that can't be shared?

I did not read for pleasure, even as a child. I never read for pleasure. Take this any way you will. I think about myself too much. I study myself. It sickens me. But this is all there is to me. I'm nothing else. My so-called ego is a little twisted thing that's probably not so different from yours but at the same time I can say confidently that it's active and bursting with importance and has major defeats and triumphs all the time. I have a stationary bike with a missing pedal that someone left on the street one night.

I also have my cigarettes close at hand. I want to feel like a writer and his cigarette. Except I'm out, they're gone, the pack has those little specks at the bottom that I already licked out of existence, and I'm tempted to smell the dead man's breath for a taste of whatever's there, the cigar he smoked a week ago in London.

All through the day I became more convinced I could not do it. Then I did it. Now I have to remember why.

I thought I would spend whatever number of years it takes to write ten thousand pages and then you would have the record, the literature of a life awake and asleep, because dreams too, and little stabs of memory, and all the pitiful habits and concealments, and all the things around me would be included, noises in the street, but I understand for the first time, now, this minute, that all the thinking and writing in the world will not describe what I felt in the awful moment when I fired the gun and saw him fall. So what is left that's worth the telling?

2

The car crossed the avenue into the West Side and had to slow down at once, moving through the crosswalk against the light, shedding waves of pedestrians.

Torval's voice reported a water-main break somewhere up ahead.

Eric saw his security aides, one to each side of the limo, walking at a calculated pace and wearing similar outfits of dark blazer, gray trousers and turtleneck shirt.

One of the screens showed a column of rusty sludge geysering high from a hole in the ground. He felt good about this. The other screens showed money moving. There were numbers gliding horizontally and bar charts pumping up and down. He knew there was something no one had detected, a pattern latent in nature itself, a leap of pictorial language that went beyond the standard models of technical analysis and out-predicted even the arcane charting of his own followers in the field. There had to be a way to explain the yen.

He was hungry, he was half starved. There were days

when he wanted to eat all the time, talk to people's faces, live in meat space. He stopped looking at computer screens and turned to the street. This was the diamond district and he lowered the window to a scene that was rocking with commerce. Nearly every store had jewelry on display and shoppers worked both sides of the street, slipping between armored bank trucks and private security vans to look at fine Swiss watches and eat in the kosher luncheonette.

The car moved at an inchworm creep.

Hasidim in frock coats and tall felt hats stood in doorways talking, men with rimless spectacles and coarse white beards, exempt from the tremor of the street. Hundreds of millions of dollars a day moved back and forth behind the walls, a form of money so obsolete Eric didn't know how to think about it. It was hard, shiny, faceted. It was everything he'd left behind or never encountered, cut and polished, intensely three-dimensional. People wore it and flashed it. They took it off to go to bed or have sex and they put it on to have sex or die in. They wore it dead and buried.

Hasidim walked along the street, younger men in dark suits and important fedoras, faces pale and blank, men who only saw each other, he thought, as they disappeared into storefronts or down the subway steps. He knew the traders and gem cutters were in the back rooms and wondered whether deals were still made in doorways with a handshake and a Yiddish blessing. In the grain of the street he sensed the Lower East Side of the 1920s and the

64

diamond centers of Europe before the second war, Amsterdam and Antwerp. He knew some history. He saw a woman seated on the sidewalk begging, a baby in her arms. She spoke a language he didn't recognize. He knew some languages but not this one. She seemed rooted to that plot of concrete. Maybe her baby had been born there, under the No Parking sign. FedEx trucks and UPS. Black men wore signboards and spoke in African murmurs. Cash for gold and diamonds. Rings, coins, pearls, wholesale jewelry, antique jewelry. This was the souk, the shtetl. Here were the hagglers and talebearers, the scrapmongers, the dealers in stray talk. The street was an offense to the truth of the future. But he responded to it. He felt it enter every receptor and vault electrically to his brain.

The car stopped dead and he got out and stretched. Traffic ahead was a long liquid shimmer of idling metal. He saw Torval walking toward him.

"Imperative that we reroute."

"The situation is what."

"This. We have flood conditions in the streets ahead. State of chaos. This. The question of the president and his whereabouts. He is fluid. He is moving. And wherever he goes, our satellite receiver reports a ripple effect in the traffic that causes mass paralysis. This also. There is a funeral proceeding slowly downtown and now deflecting westward. Many vehicles, numerous mourners on foot. And finally this. We have a report of imminent activity in the area."

"Activity."

"Imminent. Nature as yet unknown. The complex says, Use caution."

The man waited for a response. Eric was looking past him at a large shop window, one of the few on the street not showing rows of precious metal set with gems. He felt the street around him, unremitting, people moving past each other in coded moments of gesture and dance. They tried to walk without breaking stride because breaking stride is well-meaning and weak but they were forced sometimes to sidestep and even pause and they almost always averted their eyes. Eye contact was a delicate matter. A quarter second of a shared glance was a violation of agreements that made the city operational. Who steps aside for whom, who looks or does not look at whom, what level of umbrage does a brush or a touch constitute? No one wanted to be touched. There was a pact of untouchability. Even here, in the huddle of old cultures, tactile and close-woven, with passersby mixed in, and security guards, and shoppers pressed to windows, and wandering fools, people did not touch each other.

He stood in the poetry alcove at the Gotham Book Mart, leafing through chapbooks. He browsed lean books always, half a fingerbreadth or less, choosing poems to read based on length and width. He looked for poems of four, five, six lines. He scrutinized such poems, thinking into every intimation, and his feelings seemed to float in the white space around the lines. There were marks on the page and there was the page. The white was vital to the soul of the poem.

66

Klaxons sounded to the west, the electric knell of emergency vehicles that were sometimes still called ambulances, fixed in stagnant traffic.

A woman moved past, behind him, and he turned to look, too late, not sure how he knew it was a woman. He didn't see her enter the back room but knew she had. He also knew he had to follow.

Torval had not come into the bookstore with him. One of the aides was stationed near the front door, the female of the set, eyes rising briefly from the book in her hands.

He passed through the doorway into the back room, where several customers disentombed lost novels from the deep shelves. There was a woman among them and he only had to glance at her to know she was not the one he was looking for. How did he know this? He didn't but did. He checked the offices and staff toilet and then saw there were two doorways to this part of the shop. When he'd entered one, she'd left by the other, the woman he was looking for.

He went back to the main room and stood on the old floorboards, among the unpacked boxes, in the redolence of faded decades, scanning the area. She wasn't among the customers and staff. He realized his bodyguard was smiling at him, a black woman with a striking face, letting her eyes range playfully toward the door to her right. He walked over there and opened the door to a hallway that had stacks of books on one wall, photographs of sociopath poets on the other. A flight of stairs led to the gallery above the main floor and a woman sat on the stairs, unmistakably the one. There was a quality discernible in her repose, a lightness of bearing, and then he saw who she was. She was Elise Shifrin, his wife, reading a book of poems.

He said, "Recite to me."

She looked up and smiled. He knelt on the step beneath her and put his hands on her ankles, admiring her milky eyes above the headband of the book.

"Where is your necktie?" she said.

"Had my checkup. Saw my heart on a screen."

He ran his hands up her calves to the rills behind the knees.

"I don't like saying this."

"But."

"You smell of sex."

"That's my doctor's appointment you smell."

"I smell sex all over you."

"It's what. It's hunger you smell," he said. "I want to eat lunch. You want to eat lunch. We're people in the world. We need to eat and talk."

He held her hand and they moved single file through groggy traffic to the luncheonette across the street. A man sold watches from a bath towel spread across the pavement. The long room was thick with bodies and noise and he pushed past the take-out crowd and found seats at the counter.

"I'm not sure how hungry I am."

"Eat. You'll find out," he said. "Speaking of sex."

"We've been married only weeks. Barely weeks."

"Everything is barely weeks. Everything is days. We have minutes to live."

"We don't want to start counting the times, do we? Or having solemn discussions on the subject."

"No. We want to do it."

"And we will. We shall."

"We want to have it," he said.

"Sex."

"Yes. Because there isn't time not to have it. Time is a thing that grows scarcer every day. What. You don't know this?"

She looked at the menu that extended across the upper wall and seemed discouraged by its scope and mood. He cited aloud certain items he thought she might like to eat. Not that he knew what she ate.

There was a cross-roar of accents and languages and a counterman announcing food orders on a loudspeaker. Horns were blowing in the street.

"I like that bookshop. Do you know why?" she said. "Because it's semi-underground."

"You feel hidden. You like to hide. From what?"

Men talked business in tattoo raps, in formally metered chant accompanied by the clang of flatware.

"Sometimes only noise," she said, leaning into him, whispering the words cheerfully.

"You were one of those silent wistful children. Glued to the shadows."

"And you?"

"I don't know. I don't think about it."

"Think about one thing and tell me what it was."

"All right. One thing. When I was four," he said, "I figured out how much I'd weigh on each of the planets in the solar system."

"That's nice. Oh I like that," she said and kissed the side of his head, a bit maternally. "Such science and ego combined." And she laughed now, lingeringly, as he gave the counterman their orders.

An amplified voice leaked from a tour bus stuck in traffic.

"When are we going to the lake?"

"Fuck the lake."

"I thought we liked it there. After all the planning, all the construction. To get away, be alone together. It's quiet at the lake."

"It's quiet in town."

"Where we live, yes, I suppose. High enough, far enough. What about your car? Not so quiet surely. You spend a lot of time there."

"I had the car prousted."

"Yes?"

"The way they build a stretch is this. They take a vehicle's base unit and cut it in half with a huge throbbing buzz-saw device. Then they add a segment to lengthen the chassis by ten, eleven, twelve feet. Whatever desired dimension. Twenty-two feet if you like. While they were doing this to my car, I sent word that they had to proust it, cork-line it against street noise."

"That's lovely actually. I love that."

70

They were talking, they were pressed together nestling. He told himself this was his wife.

"The vehicle is armored of course. This complicated the cork-lining. But they managed in the end. It's a gesture. It's a thing a man does."

"Did it work?"

"How could it work? No. The city eats and sleeps noise. It makes noise out of every century. It makes the same noises it made in the seventeenth century along with all the noises that have evolved since then. No. But I don't mind the noise. The noise energizes me. The important thing is that it's there."

"The cork."

"That's right. The cork. This is what finally matters."

Torval was not in sight. He spotted the male body-guard standing near the cash register, appearing to study a menu. He wanted to understand why cash registers were not confined to display cases in a museum of cash registers in Philadelphia or Zurich.

Elise looked into her bowl of soup, bobbing with life forms.

"Is this what I wanted?"

"Tell me what you wanted."

"Duck consommé with an herb twist."

She said this self-mockingly, affecting an accent that was extraterritorial and only slightly more elevated than her normal system of inflection. He looked at her closely, expecting to admire the arched nostrils and the fine slight veer along the ridge of the nose. But he found himself thinking that maybe she wasn't beautiful after all. Maybe she missed. It was a stab of awareness. Maybe she was middling, desperately unexceptional. She was better-looking back in the bookstore when he'd thought she was someone else. He began to understand that they'd invented her beauty together, conspiring to assemble a fiction that worked to their mutual maneuverability and delight. They'd married in the shroud of this unspoken accord. They needed the final term in the series. She was rich, he was rich; she was heir-apparent, he was self-made; she was cultured, he was ruthless; she was brittle, he was strong; she was gifted, he was brilliant; she was beautiful. This was the core of their understanding, the thing they needed to believe before they could be a couple.

She held the soup spoon above the bowl, motionless, while she formulated a thought.

"It's true, you know. You do actually reek of sexual discharge," she said, making a point of looking into the soup.

"It's not the sex you think I've had. It's the sex I want. That's what you smell on me. Because the more I look at you, the more I know about us both."

"Tell me what that means. Or don't. No, don't."

"And the more I want to have sex with you. Because there's a certain kind of sex that has an element of cleansing. It's the antidote to disillusion. The counterpoison."

"You need to be inflamed, don't you? This is your element."

He wanted to bite her lower lip, seize it between his

teeth and bite down just hard enough to draw an erotic drop of blood.

"Where were you going," he said, "after the bookstore? Because there's a hotel."

"I was going to the bookstore. Period. I was in the bookstore. I was happy there. Where were you going?"

"To get a haircut."

She put a hand to his face and looked somber and complicated.

"Do you need a haircut?"

"I need anything you can give me."

"Be nice," she said.

"I need all the meanings of inflamed. There's a hotel just across the avenue. We can start over. Or finish with intense feeling. That's one of the meanings. To arouse to passionate feeling. We can finish what we barely started. Two hotels in fact. We have a choice."

"I don't think I want to pursue this."

"No, you don't. You wouldn't."

"Be nice to me," she said.

He waved his chopped liver sandwich, then took a loud bite, chewing and talking, and helped himself to her soup.

"Someday you'll be a grown-up," he said, "and then your mother will have no one to talk to."

Something was happening behind them. The nearest counterman spoke a line in Spanish that included the word rat. Eric swung around on his stool and saw two men in gray spandex standing in the narrow aisle between the counter and the tables. They stood motionless back to back, right arms raised, each man holding a rat by the tail. They began to shout something he could not make out. The rats were alive, forelegs pedaling, and he was fascinated, losing all sense of Elise. He wanted to understand what the men were saying and doing. They were young, in full body suits, rat suits, he realized, blocking the way to the door. He faced the long mirror on the far wall and could see most of the room, either reflected or direct, and behind him the countermen in baseball caps were arrayed in a state of thoughtful pause.

The two men separated, taking several long strides in opposite directions, and began to swing the rats over their heads, voices out of sync, shouting something about *a specter*. The face of the man who sliced pastrami hovered above his machine, eyes undecided, and the patrons didn't know how to react. Then they did, half frantic, ducking the arc of the circulating rats. A couple of people pushed through the kitchen door, disappearing, and general movement ensued, with toppled chairs and bodies spinning off the stools.

Eric was rapt. He was held nearly spellbound. He admired this thing, whatever it was. The bodyguard was at the counter, speaking into his lapel. Eric extended an arm, indicating there was no need for the man to take action. Let it express itself. People called out threats and curses that overwhelmed the voices of the two young men. He watched the nearest guy get jumpy, eyes beginning to drift. The threats sounded ancient and formulaic, one phrase eliciting the next, and even the remarks in English had an epic tenor, deathly and stretchable. He wanted to talk to the guy, ask him what the occasion was, the mission, the cause.

The countermen were armed by now with cutlery.

Then the men flung the rats, stilling the room again. The animals tail-whipped through the air, hitting and rebounding off assorted surfaces and skimming tabletops on their backs, momentum-driven, two lurid furballs running up the walls, emitting a mewl and squeak, and the men ran too, taking their shout out to the street with them, their slogan or warning or incantation.

On the other side of Sixth Avenue, the car moved slowly past the brokerage house on the corner. There were cubicles exposed at street level, men and women watching screens, and he felt the safety of their circumstance, the fastness, the involution of it, their curling embryonic ingrowth, secret and creaturely. He thought of the people who used to visit his website back in the days when he was forecasting stocks, when forecasting was pure power, when he'd tout a technology stock or bless an entire sector and automatically cause doublings in share price and the shifting of worldviews, when he was effectively making history, before history became monotonous and slobbering, yielding to his search for something purer, for techniques of charting that predicted the movements of money itself. He traded in currencies from every sort of territorial entity, modern democratic nations and dusty sultanates, paranoid people's republics, hellhole rebel states run by stoned boys.

He found beauty and precision here, hidden rhythms in the fluctuations of a given currency.

He'd left the luncheonette with half a sandwich still in hand. He was eating it now and listening to ecstatic rap on the sound system, the voice of Brutha Fez, with a Bedouin fiddle as sole accompaniment. But an image on one of the onboard screens distracted him. It was the president in his limousine, visible from the waist up. This was a feature of the Midwood administration, the chief executive on live videostream, accessible worldwide. Eric studied the man. He watched for ten motionless minutes. He didn't move and neither did the president, except reflexively, and neither did the traffic in either location. The president was in shirtsleeves, sitting in a quotidian stupor. He twitched once, blinked a few times. His gaze was empty, without direction or content. There was an air of eternal flybuzz boredom. He did not scratch or yawn and began to resemble a person sitting in an offstage lounge waiting to do a guest spot on TV. Only it was eerier and deeper than that because his eyes carried no sign of immanence, of vital occupancy, and because he seemed to exist in some little hollow of nontime, and because he was the president. Eric hated him for that. He'd talked to him several times. He'd waited in the yellow reception room in the west wing. He'd advised him on matters of some importance and had to stand where someone asked him to stand while someone else took pictures. He hated Midwood for

76

being omnipresent, as he himself used to be. He hated him for being the object of a credible threat to his safety. And he hated and mocked him for his gynecoid upper body with its swag of dangling mammaries under the sheer white shirt. He looked vengefully at the screen, thinking the image did the president every justice. He was the undead. He lived in a state of occult repose, waiting to be reanimated.

"We want to think about the art of money-making," she said.

She was sitting in the rear seat, his seat, the club chair, and he looked at her and waited.

"The Greeks have a word for it."

He waited.

"*Chrimatistikós*," she said. "But we have to give the word a little leeway. Adapt it to the current situation. Because money has taken a turn. All wealth has become wealth for its own sake. There's no other kind of enormous wealth. Money has lost its narrative quality the way painting did once upon a time. Money is talking to itself."

She usually wore a beret but was bareheaded today, Vija Kinski, a small woman in a button-down business shirt, an old embroidered vest and a long pleated skirt of a thousand launderings, his chief of theory, late for their weekly meeting.

"And property follows of course. The concept of property is changing by the day, by the hour. The enormous expenditures that people make for land and houses and

77

boats and planes. This has nothing to do with traditional self-assurances, okay. Property is no longer about power, personality and command. It's not about vulgar display or tasteful display. Because it no longer has weight or shape. The only thing that matters is the price you pay. Yourself, Eric, think. What did you buy for your one hundred and four million dollars? Not dozens of rooms, incomparable views, private elevators. Not the rotating bedroom and computerized bed. Not the swimming pool or the shark. Was it air rights? The regulating sensors and software? Not the mirrors that tell you how you feel when you look at yourself in the morning. You paid the money for the number itself. One hundred and four million. This is what you bought. And it's worth it. The number justifies itself."

The car sat in stationary traffic halfway between the avenues, where Kinski had boarded, emerging from the Church of Saint Mary the Virgin. This was curious but maybe it wasn't. He faced her from the jump seat, wondering why he didn't know how old she was. Her hair was smoky gray and looked lightning-struck, withered and singed, but her face was barely marked except for a large mole high on her cheek.

"Oh and this car, which I love. The glow of the screens. I love the screens. The glow of cyber-capital. So radiant and seductive. I understand none of it."

She spoke in near whispers and wore a persistent smile, with cryptic variations.

"But you know how shameless I am in the presence of anything that calls itself an idea. The idea is time. Living in

78

the future. Look at those numbers running. Money makes time. It used to be the other way around. Clock time accelerated the rise of capitalism. People stopped thinking about eternity. They began to concentrate on hours, measurable hours, man-hours, using labor more efficiently."

He said, "There's something I want to show you."

"Wait. I'm thinking."

He waited. Her smile was slightly twisted.

"It's cyber-capital that creates the future. What is the measurement called a nanosecond?"

"Ten to the minus ninth power."

"This is what."

"One billionth of a second," he said.

"I understand none of this. But it tells me how rigorous we need to be in order to take adequate measure of the world around us."

"There are zeptoseconds."

"Good. I'm glad."

"Yoctoseconds. One septillionth of a second."

"Because time is a corporate asset now. It belongs to the free market system. The present is harder to find. It is being sucked out of the world to make way for the future of uncontrolled markets and huge investment potential. The future becomes insistent. This is why something will happen soon, maybe today," she said, looking slyly into her hands. "To correct the acceleration of time. Bring nature back to normal, more or less."

The south side of the street was nearly empty of pedestrians. He led her out of the car and onto the sidewalk, where they were able to get a partial view of the electronic display of market information, the moving message units that streaked across the face of an office tower on the other side of Broadway. Kinski was transfixed. This was very different from the relaxed news reports that wrapped around the old Times Tower a few blocks south of here. These were three tiers of data running concurrently and swiftly about a hundred feet above the street. Financial news, stock prices, currency markets. The action was unflagging. The hellbent sprint of numbers and symbols, the fractions, decimals, stylized dollar signs, the streaming release of words, of multinational news, all too fleet to be absorbed. But he knew that Kinski was absorbing it.

He stood behind her, pointing over her shoulder. Beneath the data strips, or tickers, there were fixed digits marking the time in the major cities of the world. He knew what she was thinking. Never mind the speed that makes it hard to follow what passes before the eye. The speed is the point. Never mind the urgent and endless replenishment, the way data dissolves at one end of the series just as it takes shape at the other. This is the point, the thrust, the future. We are not witnessing the flow of information so much as pure spectacle, or information made sacred, ritually unreadable. The small monitors of the office, home and car become a kind of idolatry here, where crowds might gather in astonishment.

She said, "Does it ever stop? Does it slow down? Of course not. Why should it? Fantastic."

He saw a familiar name flash across the news ticker.

Kaganovich. But he missed the context. Traffic began to move, barely, and they went back to the car with the two bodyguards providing discreet escort. He sat on the banquette this time, facing the visual displays, and learned that the context was the death of Nikolai Kaganovich, a man of swaggering wealth and shady reputation, owner of Russia's largest media conglomerate, with interests that ranged from sex magazines to satellite operations.

He respected Kaganovich. The man was shrewd and tough, cruel in the best sense. He and Nikolai had been friends, he told Kinski. He took a bottle of blood orange vodka out of the cooler and poured two short glasses, neat, and they watched coverage of the event on several screens.

She flushed a little, sipping her drink.

The man lay facedown in the mud in front of his dacha outside Moscow, shot numerous times just after returning from a trip to Albania Online, where he'd set up a cable TV network and signed agreements for a theme park in Tirana, the capital.

Eric and Nikolai had tracked wild boar in Siberia. He told Kinski about this. They'd seen a tiger in the distance, a glimpse, a sting of pure transcendence, outside all previous experience. He described the moment to her, the precious sense of last life, a species in peril, and the vastness of the silence around them. They remained motionless, the two men, long after the animal had vanished. The sight of the tiger aflame in high snow made them feel bound to an unspoken code, a brotherhood of beauty and loss.

But he was glad to see the man dead in the mud. The

reporter kept using the word dacha. He stood at an angle to the camera, allowing a clear look at the villa, the dacha, through an alley of pines. On another screen a commentator made vague references to unsavory business associates, to anti-globalist elements and local wars. Then she talked about the dacha. Found dead facedown outside his dacha. They searched for security in the word, self-confidence. It was all they knew about the man and the crime, something Russian, that he was dead outside his dacha outside Moscow.

Eric felt good about it, seeing him there, unnumbered bullet wounds to the body and head. It was a quiet contentment, an easing of some unspecifiable pressure in the shoulders and chest. It relaxed him, the death of Nikolai Kaganovich. He didn't say this to Kinski. Then he did. Why not? She was his chief of theory. Let her theorize.

"Your genius and your animus have always been fully linked," she said. "Your mind thrives on ill will toward others. So does your body, I think. Bad blood makes for long life. He was a rival in some sense, yes? He was physically strong perhaps. He had a large personality. Filthy rich, this chap. Women in his soup. Reasons enough to feel a sneaky sort of euphoria when the man dies horribly. There are always, always reasons. Don't examine the matter," she said. "He died so you can live."

The car reached the corner and stopped. There were tourists pressing through the theater district in all the words that make a multitude. They moved in swirls and drifts, shuffling in and out of megastores and circling vendors' carts. They stood in a convoluted line, folded back against itself, for cut-rate tickets to Broadway shows. Eric watched them cross the street, stunted humans in the shadow of the underwear gods that adorned the soaring billboards. These were figures beyond gender and procreation, enchanted women in men's shorts, beyond commerce, even, men immortal in their muscle tone, in the clustered bulge at the crotchline.

Heavy trucks went downtown bouncing, headed to the garment district or the meatpacking docks, and nobody saw them. They saw the cockney selling children's books from a cardboard box, making his pitch from his knees. Eric thought they were the same thing, these two, and the old Chinese was the same, doing acupoint massage, and the repair crew passing fiber-optic cable down a manhole from an enormous yellow spool. He thought about the amassments, the material crush, days and nights of bumper to bumper, red light, green light, the fixedness of things, the obsolescences, going mostly unseen. They saw the old man do his therapeutic massage, working a woman's back and temples as she sat on a bench, her face pressed to a raised cushion attached to a makeshift frame. They read the handwritten sign, relief from fatigue and panic. How things persist, the habits of gravity and time, in this new and fluid reality. The cockney from his knees said, I don't ask you where you get your money, don't ask me where I get my books. They stopped and looked, browsing his cardboard box. The old Chinese stood erect, kneading the woman's acupuncture points, thumbing the furrows behind her ears.

Eric saw people stop at the foreign exchange booth on the southeast corner. This prompted him to open the sunroof and stick his head outside, able to get an unobstructed look at the currency prices skimming across the building just ahead. The yen was climbing, still, trading up against the dollar.

He sat in the jump seat facing Kinski and told her what the situation was, broadly, that he was borrowing yen at extremely low interest rates and using this money to speculate heavily in stocks that would yield potentially high returns.

"Please. Means nothing to me."

But the stronger the yen became, the more money he needed to pay back the loan.

"Stop. I'm lost."

He kept doing this because he knew the yen could not go any higher. He explained that there were levels it could not reach. The market knew this. There were oscillations and shocks that the market tolerated to a certain point but not beyond. The yen itself knew it could not go higher. But it did go higher, time and again.

She held the vodka glass between her palms, rolling it while she thought. He waited. She wore tiny tasseled loafers and white ankle socks.

"The wise course would be to back down, stand off. You are being advised to do this," she said.

"Yes."

"But there's something you know. You know the yen can't go any higher. And if you know something and don't act upon it, then you didn't know it in the first place. There is a piece of Chinese wisdom," she said. "To know and not to act is not to know."

He loved Vija Kinski.

"To pull back now would not be authentic. It would be a quotation from other people's lives. A paraphrase of a sensible text that wants you to believe there are plausible realities, okay, that can be traced and analyzed."

"When in fact what."

"That wants you to believe there are foreseeable trends and forces. When in fact it's all random phenomena. You apply mathematics and other disciplines, yes. But in the end you're dealing with a system that's out of control. Hysteria at high speeds, day to day, minute to minute. People in free societies don't have to fear the pathology of the state. We create our own frenzy, our own mass convulsions, driven by thinking machines that we have no final authority over. The frenzy is barely noticeable most of the time. It's simply how we live."

She finished with a laugh. Yes, he admired her gift for cogent speech, shapely and persuasive, with a rubbed finish. This is what he wanted from her. Organized thoughts, challenging remarks. But there was something dirty in her laugh. It was scornful and coarse.

"Of course you know this," she said.

He did and did not. Not to this nihilistic degree. Not to the point where all judgments are baseless.

"There's an order at some deep level," he said. "A pattern that wants to be seen."

"Then see it."

He heard voices in the distance.

"I always have. But it's been elusive in this instance. My experts have struggled and just about given up. I've been working on it, sleeping on it, not sleeping on it. There's a common surface, an affinity between market movements and the natural world."

"An aesthetics of interaction."

"Yes. But in this case I'm beginning to doubt I'll ever find it."

"Doubt. What is doubt? You don't believe in doubt. You've told me this. Computer power eliminates doubt. All doubt rises from past experience. But the past is disappearing. We used to know the past but not the future. This is changing," she said. "We need a new theory of time."

The car moved forward, clearing one stream of southbound traffic but stopping short of the next, suspended in the compressed space where Seventh Avenue and Broadway begin to intersect. He heard the voices more clearly now, carrying across the traffic, and saw people running, the vanguard of a crowd, coming this way, and others spilling off the sidewalks, startled and confused, and a styrofoam rat twenty feet tall dodging taxis in the street.

He stuck his head out the sunroof and watched. What was happening? It was hard to say.

Both avenues were impacted now, vehicles blocked

and people everywhere. Pedestrians fled into the cross streets, outside the runners' line of advance. It wasn't a line but a warp in the crowd. There were runners and others, those trying to run, angling for space to move freely, hand-paddling past knotted bodies.

He wanted to understand, to separate one thing from another through detailed observation. There were horns and sirens sounding. The massed voices called above the ambient splash of the crowd. This only made it harder to see.

He was looking south, into the heart of Times Square. He heard plate glass breaking, falling in sheets to the pavement. There was an isolated disturbance outside the Nasdaq Center a few blocks away. Shapes and colors were shifting, a slow lean of bodies. They were swarming the entrance and he imagined pandemonium inside, people racing through galleries surfaced in information. They would break into control rooms, attack the video wall and logo ticker.

Directly in front of him, what? People on the traffic island buying discount theater tickets. They were still in line, most of them, not willing to lose their places, the only image in broad view that was not raw and tossing.

The voices carried through bullhorns in intonations of chant, the same tonal contour he'd heard in the shouts of the young men at lunch. The styrofoam rat was on the sidewalk now, carried on a litter shouldered by four or five people in rodent spandex, coming this way.

He saw Torval in the street with the two bodyguards,

all three swiveling at different degrees of speed to scan the area, impressively. The woman looked Egyptian in profile, Middle Kingdom, leaning toward her left breast to speak into the wearable phone. It was time to retire the word phone.

Runners began to emerge from both sides of the ticket outlet, most in ski masks, some pausing when they saw the car. The car made them pause. There were police vehicles racing and skidding to the edge of the cross streets. He began to feel involved. A bus deposited figures in riot gear, wearing snouted masks.

A driver stood by his taxi, smoking, arms crossed at his chest, South Asian and patiently waiting, in the world city, for things to make some sense.

There were people approaching the car. Who were they? They were protesters, anarchists, whoever they were, a form of street theater, or adepts of sheer rampage. The car was hemmed in, of course, enveloped by paralysis, with vehicles on three sides and the ticket booths on the fourth. He saw Torval confront a man carrying a brick. He dropped him cold with a right cross. Eric decided to admire this.

Then Torval looked up at him. A kid on a skateboard flew past, bouncing off the windshield of a police cruiser. It was clear what his chief of security wanted him to do. The two men stared balefully at each other for a long moment. Then Eric lowered himself into the body of the car and eased the sunroof shut.

*   *   *

He said, "What?"

"It pretends not to see the horror and death at the end of the schemes it builds. This is a protest against the future. They want to hold off the future. They want to normalize it, keep it from overwhelming the present."

There were cars burning in the street, metal hissing and spitting, and stunned figures in slow motion, in tides of smoke, wandering through the mass of vehicles and bodies, and others everywhere running, and a cop down, genuflected, outside a fast food shop.

"The future is always a wholeness, a sameness. We're all tall and happy there," she said. "This is why the future fails. It always fails. It can never be the cruel happy place we want to make it."

Someone flung a trash can at the rear window. Kinski flinched but barely. To the immediate west, just across Broadway, the protesters created barricades of burning tires. All along there'd seemed a scheme, a destination. Police fired rubber bullets through the smoke, which began to drift high above the billboards. Other police stood a few feet away, helping Eric's security detail protect the car. He didn't know how he felt about this.

"How will we know when the global era officially ends?" He waited.

"When stretch limousines begin to disappear from the streets of Manhattan."

Men were urinating on the car. Women pitched sand-filled soda bottles.

"This is controlled anger, I would say. But what would

happen if they knew that the head of Packer Capital was in the car?"

She said this evilly, eyes alight. The protesters' eyes were blazing between the red-and-black bandannas they wore across their heads and faces. Did he envy them? The shatterproof windows showed hairline fractures and maybe he thought he'd like to be out there, mangling and smashing.

"They are working with you, these people. They are acting on your terms," she said. "And if they kill you, it's only because you permit it, in your sweet sufferance, as a way to re-emphasize the idea we all live under."

"What idea?"

The rocking became worse and he watched her follow her glass from side to side before she was able to take a sip.

"Destruction," she said.

On one of the screens he saw figures descending a vertical surface. It took him a moment to understand that they were rappelling down the facade of the building just ahead, where the market tickers were located.

"You know what anarchists have always believed."

"Yes."

"Tell me," she said.

"The urge to destroy is a creative urge."

"This is also the hallmark of capitalist thought. Enforced destruction. Old industries have to be harshly eliminated. New markets have to be forcibly claimed.

Old markets have to be re-exploited. Destroy the past, make the future."

Her smile was private, as always, and a minor muscle twitched at a corner of her mouth. She was not in the habit of revealing sympathies or disaffections. She had no capacity for either, he'd thought, but wondered now if he'd been wrong about that.

They were spray-painting the car, doing adagios on their skateboards. Across the avenue the men dangling from belayed ropes were trying to kick in windows. The tower carried the name of a major investment bank, the lettering modestly sized beneath a sprawling map of the world, and the stock prices danced through the fading light.

There were many arrests, people from forty countries, heads bloodied, ski masks in hand. They did not want to relinquish their masks. He saw a woman take off her mask, pull it off cursing, a cop prodding her ribs with his baton, and she swung the mask backhand, swatting his visored helmet as they passed out of camera range, and all the screens tossed to the heaving of the car.

His own image caught his eye, live on the oval screen beneath the spycam. Some seconds passed. He saw himself recoil in shock. More time passed. He felt suspended, waiting. Then there was a detonation, loud and deep, near enough to consume all the information around him. He recoiled in shock. Everyone did. The phrase was part of the gesture, the familiar expression, embodied in the motion of the head and limbs. He recoiled in shock. The phrase reverberated in the body.

The car stopped rocking. There was a general sense of contemplation. They were all of them out there bonded now in a second level of engagement.

The bomb had been set off just outside the investment bank. He saw shadowy footage on another screen, figures running at digital speed down a corridor, stutter-running, with readouts of tenths of seconds. It was surveillance coverage from cameras in the tower. The protesters were storming the building, busting through the crumpled entrance and commanding the elevators and hallways.

The struggle resumed outside with the police turning fire hoses on the burning barricades and the protesters chanting anew, alive, restored to fearlessness and moral force.

But they seemed to be done with his car at last.

They sat quietly for a moment.

He said, "Did you see that?"

"Yes, I did. What was it?"

He said, "I'm sitting. We're talking. I look at the screen. Then suddenly."

"You recoil in shock."

"Yes."

"Then the blast."

"Yes."

"Has this happened, I wonder, before?"

"Yes. I had our computer security tested."

"Nothing amiss."

"No. Not that anyone, anyway, could produce such an effect. Could anticipate such a thing."

"You recoiled in shock."

"On-screen."

"Then the blast. And then."

"Recoiled for real," he said.

"Whatever that might possibly mean."

She worked her mole. She fingered the mole on her cheek, twisting it as she thought. He sat and waited.

"This is the thing about genius," she said. "Genius alters the terms of its habitat."

He liked that but wanted more.

"Think of it this way. There are rare minds operating, a few, here and there, the polymath, the true futurist. A consciousness such as yours, hypermaniacal, may have contact points beyond the general perception."

He waited.

"Technology is crucial to civilization why? Because it helps us make our fate. We don't need God or miracles or the flight of the bumble bee. But it is also crouched and undecidable. It can go either way."

The tickers went dark on the face of the tower under assault.

"You've been talking about the future being impatient. Pressing upon us."

"That was theory. I deal in theory," she said sharply.

He turned away from her and watched the screens. The top tier of the electronic display across the avenue showed this message now:

A SPECTER IS HAUNTING THE WORLD—
THE SPECTER OF CAPITALISM

He recognized the variation on the famous first sentence of *The Communist Manifesto* in which Europe is haunted by the specter of communism, circa 1850.

They were confused and wrongheaded. But his respect for the protesters' ingenuity grew more certain. He slid open the sunroof and poked his head into the smoke and gas, with burning rubber thick in the air, and he thought he was an astronaut come upon a planet of pure flatus. It was bracing. A figure in a motorcycle helmet mounted the hood and began crawling across the roof of the car. Torval reached up and scraped him off. He tossed him to the ground, where the bodyguards took over. They had to use a stun gun to subdue him and the voltage delivered the man to another dimension. Eric barely noticed the crackling sound and the arced charge of current that jumped the gap between electrodes. He was watching the second ticker begin to operate, words racing north to south.

A RAT BECAME THE UNIT OF CURRENCY

It took him a moment to absorb the words and identify the line. He knew the line of course. It was out of a poem he'd been reading lately, one of the few longer poems he'd chosen to investigate, a line, half a line from the chronicle of a city under siege.

It was exhilarating, his head in the fumes, to see the struggle and ruin around him, the gassed men and women in their defiance, waving looted Nasdaq T-shirts, and to realize they'd been reading the same poetry he'd been reading.

He sat down long enough to take a web phone out of a slot and execute an order for more yen. He borrowed yen in dumbfounding amounts. He wanted all the yen there was.

Then he put his head outside again to watch the words leap repeatedly across the shiny gray facade. The police launched a counter-assault on the tower, led by a special unit. He liked special units. They wore bullet helmets and dark slickers, men with automatic weapons that were skeleton guns, all framework and no body.

Something else was happening. There was a shift, a break in space. Again he wasn't sure what he was seeing, only thirty yards away but unreliable, delusional, where a man sat on the sidewalk with legs crossed, trembling in a length of braided flame.

He was close enough to see that the man wore glasses. There was a man on fire. People turned away crouching or stood with hands to faces, spun and crouched and went to their knees, or walked past unaware, ran past in the shuffle and smoke without noticing, or watched spell-struck, bodies going slack, faces round and dumb.

When the wind blew, gusting suddenly, the flames dipped and flattened but the man remained rigid, his face unobscured, and they saw his glasses melt into his eyes.

The sound of moaning began to spread. A man stood wailing. Two women sat on the curbstone wailing. They draped their arms over their heads and faces. Another woman wanted to snuff the fire but only got close enough to wave her jacket at the man, careful not to hit him. He was rocking slightly and his head was burning independent of the body. There was a break in the flames.

His shirt was assumed, it was received spiritually into the air in the form of shreds of smoky matter, and his skin went dark and bubbly and this is what they began to smell now, burnt flesh mixed with gasoline.

A jerry can stood upright close to his knee and it was also burning, ignited when he'd set himself on fire. There were no chanting monks in ochre robes or nuns in dappled gray. It seemed he'd done this on his own.

He was young or not. He'd made the judgment out of lucid conviction. They wanted him to be young and driven by conviction. Eric believed even the police wanted this. No one wanted a deranged man. It dishonored their action, their risk, all the work they'd done together. He was not a transient in a narrow room who suffers episodes of this or that, hearing voices in his head.

Eric wanted to imagine the man's pain, his choice, the abysmal will he'd had to summon. He tried to imagine him in bed, this morning, staring sideways at a wall, thinking his way toward the moment. Did he have to go to a store and buy a box of matches? He imagined a phone call to someone far away, a mother or lover.

The cameramen moved in now, abandoning the special unit that was retaking the tower across the street. They came running to the corner, broad men in haunchy sprints, cameras bouncing on their shoulders, and they closed in tight on the burning man.

He lowered himself into the car and sat in the jump seat, facing Vija Kinski.

Even with the beatings and gassings, the jolt of explosives, even in the assault on the investment bank, he thought there was something theatrical about the protest, ingratiating, even, in the parachutes and skateboards, the styrofoam rat, in the tactical coup of reprogramming the stock tickers with poetry and Karl Marx. He thought Kinski was right when she said this was a market fantasy. There was a shadow of transaction between the demonstrators and the state. The protest was a form of systemic hygiene, purging and lubricating. It attested again, for the ten thousandth time, to the market culture's innovative brilliance, its ability to shape itself to its own flexible ends, absorbing everything around it.

Now look. A man in flames. Behind Eric all the screens were pulsing with it. And all action was at a pause, the protesters and riot police milling about and only the cameras jostling. What did this change? Everything, he thought. Kinski had been wrong. The market was not total. It could not claim this man or assimilate his act. Not such starkness and horror. This was a thing outside its reach.

He could see the coverage in her face. She was downcast. The interior of the car tapered toward the rear, lending authority to the seat she was in, normally his of course, and he knew how much she liked to sit in the glove-leather chair and glide through the city day or night speaking ex cathedra. But she was dejected now and did not look at him.

"It's not original," she said finally.

"Hey. What's original? He did it, didn't he?"

"It's an appropriation."

"He poured the gasoline and lit the match."

"All those Vietnamese monks, one after another, in all their lotus positions."

"Imagine the pain. Sit there and feel it."

"Immolating themselves endlessly."

"To say something. To make people think."

"It's not original," she said.

"Does he have to be a Buddhist to be taken seriously? He did a serious thing. He took his life. Isn't this what you have to do to show them that you're serious?"

Torval wanted to talk to him. The door was dented and bent and it took Torval a moment to work it open. Eric moved in a crouch to exit the car, passing near Kinski as he did, but she would not look at him.

*   *   *

The members of an ambulance crew moved slowly through the crowd, using their gurney to clear the way. Sirens were blowing in the cross streets.

The body had stopped burning by now and was still rigidly set in a seated position, leaking vapors and haze. The stink came and went with the wind. The wind was stronger now, storm-bearing, and there was thunder in the distance.

At the side of the car the two men were in a state of formal avoidance, looking past each other. The car sat stunned. It was slathered in red-and-black spray paint. There were dozens of bruises and punctures, long burrowing scrape marks, swaths of impact and discolor. There were places where splashes of urine were preserved in pentimento stainage beneath the flourish of graffiti.

Torval said, "Just now."

"What?"

"Report from the complex. Concerns your safety."

"Little late, are they?"

"This is specific and categorical."

"There's been a threat then."

"Assessment, credible red. Highest order of urgency. This means an incursion is already in progress."

"Now we know."

"And now we have to act on what we know."

"But we still want what we want," Eric said.

Torval adjusted his point of view. He looked at Eric. It seemed a massive transgression, violating the logic of coded glances, vocal tones and other gestural parameters of their particular terms of reference. It was the first time he'd studied Eric in such an open manner. He looked and nodded, pursuing some somber course of thought.

"We want a haircut," Eric told him.

He saw a police lieutenant carrying a walkie-talkie. What entered his mind when he saw this? He wanted to ask the man why he was still using such a contraption, still calling it what he called it, carrying the nitwit rhyme out of the age of industrial glut into smart spaces built on beams of light.

He got back in the car to wait for the long untangling of traffic. People began to move off, some with bandannas still secured against the afterburn of tear gas and the probes of police cameras. There were skirmishes taking place, a few and scattered, men and women running on broken glass that covered the sidewalks and others catcalling at the stoic cops posted on the traffic island.

He told Kinski what he'd heard.

"Do they think the threat is credible?"

"Status urgent."

She was delighted. She began to be herself again, smiling inwardly. Then she looked at him and spilled into laughter. He wasn't sure what was funny about this but found himself laughing as well. He felt defined, etched sharply. He felt a burst of self-realization that heightened and clarified.

"It's interesting, isn't it?" she said.

He waited.

102

"About men and immortality."

They covered the burnt body and wheeled it away, semi-upright, with rats in the streets and the first drops of rain coming down and the light changing radically in the preternatural way that's completely natural, of course, all the electric premonition that rides the sky being a drama of human devising.

"You live in a tower that soars to heaven and goes unpunished by God."

She found this amusing.

"And you bought an airplane. I'd nearly forgotten this. Soviet or ex-Soviet. A strategic bomber. Capable of knocking out a small city. Is this right?"

"It's an old Tu-160. NATO calls it Blackjack A. It was deployed around 1988. Carries nuclear bombs and cruise missiles," he said. "These were not included in the deal."

She clapped her hands, happy and charmed.

"But they wouldn't let you fly it. Could you fly it?"

"Could and did. They wouldn't let me fly it armed."

"Who wouldn't?"

"The State Department. The Pentagon. The Bureau of Alcohol, Tobacco and Firearms."

"The Russians?"

"What Russians? I bought it black-market and dirt cheap from a Belgian arms dealer in Kazakhstan. That's where I took the controls, for half an hour, over the desert. U.S. dollars, thirty-one million."

"Where is it now?"

"Parked in a storage facility in Arizona. Waiting for replacement parts that nobody can find. Sitting in the wind. I go out there now and then."

"To do what?"

"To look at it. It's mine," he said.

She closed her eyes and thought. The screens showed charts and graphs, market updates. She clutched one hand in the other, tightly, veins going flat and blood draining from her knuckles.

"People will not die. Isn't this the creed of the new culture? People will be absorbed in streams of information. I know nothing about this. Computers will die. They're dying in their present form. They're just about dead as distinct units. A box, a screen, a keyboard. They're melting into the texture of everyday life. This is true or not?"

"Even the word computer."

"Even the word computer sounds backward and dumb."

She opened her eyes and seemed to look right through him, speaking quietly, and he began to imagine her asquat his chest in the middle of the night, in candlelight, not sexually or demonically driven but there to speak into his fitful sleep, to trouble his dreams with her theories.

She talked. This was her job. She was born to it and got paid for it. But what did she believe? Her eyes were unrevealing. At least to him they were, faint, gray, remote to him, unalive to him, bright at times but only in the flush of an insight or conjecture. Where was her life? What did she do when she went home? Who was there besides the cat? He thought there had to be a cat. How could they talk about such things, these two? They were not qualified.

It would be a breach of trust, he thought, to ask if she had a cat, much less a husband, a lover, life insurance. What are your plans for the weekend? The question would be a form of assault. She would turn away, angry and humiliated. She was a voice with a body as afterthought, a wry smile that sailed through heavy traffic. Give her a history and she'd disappear.

"I understand none of this," she said. "Microchips so small and powerful. Humans and computers merge. This is well beyond my range. And never-ending life begins." She took a moment to look at him. "Shouldn't the glory of a great man's death argue against his dream of immortality?"

Kinski naked on his chest.

"Men think about immortality. Never mind what women think. We're too small and real to matter here," she said. "Great men historically expected to live forever even as they supervised construction of their monumental tombs on the far bank of the river, the west bank, where the sun goes down."

Kinski vivid in his nightmares, commenting on events therein.

"There you sit, of large visions and prideful acts. Why die when you can live on disk? A disk, not a tomb. An idea beyond the body. A mind that's everything you ever were and will be, but never weary or confused or impaired. It's a mystery to me, how such a thing might happen. Will it happen someday? Sooner than we think because every-thing happens sooner than we think. Later today per-haps. Maybe today is the day when everything happens, for better or worse, ka-boom, like that."

It was twilight, only dimmer, with a silvery twinge in the air, and he stood outside his car watching taxis extract themselves from the ruck. He didn't know how long it was since he'd felt so good.

How long? He didn't know.

With the currency ticker restored to normal function, the yen showed renewed strength, advancing against the dollar in microdecimal increments every sextillionth of a second. This was good. This was fine and right. It thrilled him to think in zeptoseconds and to watch the numbers in their unrelenting run. The stock ticker was also good. He watched the major issues breeze by and felt purified in nameless ways to see prices spiral into lubricious plunge. Yes, the effect on him was sexual, cunnilingual in partic-ular, and he let his head fall back and opened his mouth to the sky and rain.

The rain came washing down on the emptying breadth of Times Square with the billboards ghost-lighted now and the tire barricades nearly cleared dead ahead, leaving 47th Street open to the west. The rain was fine. The rain was dramatically right. But the threat was even better. He saw a few tourists creep along Broadway under bunched umbrellas to stare at the charred spot on the pavement where an unknown man had set fire to himself. This was grave and haunting. It was right for the moment and the day. But the credible threat was the thing that moved and quickened him. The rain on his face was good and the sour reek was fine and right, the fug of urine maturing on the body of his car, and there was trembling pleasure to be found, and joy at all misfortune, in the swift pitch of markets down. But it was the threat of death at the brink of night that spoke to him most surely about some principle of fate he'd always known would come clear in time.

Now he could begin the business of living.

PART TWO

3

She had coral brown skin and well-defined cheekbones. There was a beeswax sheen to her lips. She liked to be looked at and made the act of undressing seem proudly public, an unveiling across national borders with an element of slightly showy defiance.

She wore her ZyloFlex body armor while they had sex. This was his idea. She told him the ballistic fiber was the lightest and softest available, and the strongest as well, and also stab-resistant.

Her name was Kendra Hays and she was easy in his presence. They mock-boxed for about a second and a half. He licked her body here and there, leaving fizzes of spittle behind.

"You work out," she said.

"Six percent body fat."

"Used to be my number. Then I got lazy."

"What are you doing about it?"

"Hit the machines in the morning. Run in the park at night."

She had cinnamon skin, or russet, or a blend of copper and bronze. He wondered if she felt ordinary to herself, riding an elevator alone, thinking about lunch.

She shed the vest and took her room service scotch to the window. Her clothing was folded on a chair nearby. He wanted to spend a day in silence, in his meditation cell, just looking at her face and body, as an exercise in Tao, or fasting with the mind. He didn't ask her what she knew about the credible threat. He wasn't interested in details, not yet, and Torval wouldn't have said much, anyway, to the bodyguards.

"Where is he now?"

"Who?"

"You know."

"He's in the lobby. Torval? Watching them come and go. Danko's in the hall outside."

"Who's that?"

"Danko. My partner."

"He's new."

"I'm new. He's been watching your back for some time now, ever since those wars in the Balkans. He's a veteran."

Eric sat cross-legged on the bed popping peanuts in his mouth and watching her.

"What's he going to say to you about this?"

"Torval? Is that who you're talking about?" She was amused. "Say his name."

"What's he going to say to you?"

"Just so you're safe. That's his job," she said.

"Men get possessive. What. You don't know this?"

"I heard the rumor. But the fact is I technically speaking went off duty an hour ago. So it's basically my time we're dealing with here."

He liked her. The more he knew Torval would hate her, the more he liked her. Torval would hate her hotbloodedly for this. He'd spend weeks glaring out at her from under his stormy brows.

"Do you find this interesting?"

She said, "What?"

"Protecting someone in danger."

He wanted her to move slightly left so that her hip would catch the glow of the table lamp nearby.

"What makes you willing to do this? Take this risk."

"Maybe you're worth it," she said.

She dipped a finger in her drink, then forgot to lick it.

"Maybe it's just the pay. The pay's pretty good. The risk? I don't think about the risk. I figure the risk is yours. You're the man in the crosshairs."

She thought this was funny.

"But is it interesting?"

"It's interesting to be near a man somebody wants to kill."

"You know what they say, don't you?"

"What?"

"The logical extension of business is murder."

This was funny too.

He said, "Move a little left."

"Move a little left."

"There. Nice. Perfect."

113

Her skin was foxy brown, hair braided close to the scalp.

"What kind of weapon did he give you?"

"Stun gun. Doesn't trust me yet with deadly force."

She approached the bed and took the glass of vodka out of his hand. He could not stop tossing peanuts in his mouth.

"You ought to eat more healthy."

He said, "Today is different. How many volts at your disposal?"

"One hundred thousand. Jam your nervous system. Drop you to your knees. Like this," she said.

She poured a few drops of vodka on his genitals. It stung, it burned. She laughed when she did it and he wanted her to do it again. She poured a trickle more and bent over to lap it off, to tongue-scrub him in vodka, and then knelt astride him. She had a glass in each hand and tried to keep her balance while they bounced and laughed.

He finished off her scotch and ate peanuts by the fist-ful while she showered. He watched her shower and thought she was a woman of straps and belts. At some level she would never be naked.

Then he stood by the bed to watch her dress. She took her time, the body armor fastened across her torso, the pants about to be fastened, shoes next, and was fitting the waistband holster onto her hip when she saw him standing in his shorts.

He said, "Stun me. I mean it. Draw the gun and shoot.

I want you to do it, Kendra. Show me what it feels like. I'm looking for more. Show me something I don't know. Stun me to my DNA. Come on, do it. Click the switch. Aim and fire. I want all the volts the weapon holds. Do it. Shoot it. Now."

The car was parked outside the hotel and across the street from the Barrymore, where a group of smokers gathered at intermission, tucked under the marquee.

He sat in the car borrowing yen and watching his fund's numbers sink into the mist on several screens. Torval stood in the rain with arms folded. He was a lone figure in the street, facing a series of empty loading docks.

The yen spree was releasing Eric from the influence of his neocortex. He felt even freer than usual, attuned to the registers of his lower brain and gaining distance from the need to take inspired action, make original judgments, maintain independent principles and convictions, all the reasons why people are fucked up and birds and rats are not.

The stun gun probably helped. The voltage had jellified his musculature for ten or fifteen minutes and he'd rolled about on the hotel rug, electroconvulsive and strangely elated, deprived of his faculties of reason.

But he could think now, well enough to understand what was happening. There were currencies tumbling everywhere. Bank failures were spreading. He found the humidor and lit a cigar. Strategists could not explain the speed and depth of the fall. They opened their mouths and words came out. He knew it was the yen. His actions regarding the yen were causing storms of disorder. He was so leveraged, his firm's portfolio large and sprawling, linked crucially to the affairs of so many key institutions, all reciprocally vulnerable, that the whole system was in danger.

He smoked and watched, feeling strong, proud, stupid and superior. He was also bored and a little dismissive. They were making too much of it. He thought it would end in a day or two and he was about to code a word to the driver when he noticed that people under the marquee were staring at the car, battered and paint-sprayed.

He lowered the window and looked more closely at one of the women standing there. At first he thought it was Elise Shifrin. This is how he sometimes thought of his wife, by full name, due to her relative celebrity in the social columns and the fashion books. Then he wasn't sure who it was, either because his view was partly obstructed or because the woman in question had a cigarette in her hand.

He forced open the door and walked across the street and Torval was at his side, ably containing his rage.

"I need to know where you're going."

"Wait and learn," he said.

The woman looked away when he approached. It was Elise, noncommittally, in profile.

"You smoke since when."

She answered without turning to face him, speaking from a seeming distance.

"I took it up when I was fifteen. It's one of those things a girl takes up. It tells her she's more than a skinny body no one looks at. There's a certain drama in her life."

"She notices herself. Then other people notice her. Then she marries one of them. Then they go to dinner," he said.

Torval and Danko flanked the limo and it moved deliberately down the street in light taxi traffic, husband and wife assessing the prospects of immediate eating places. One of the screens displayed a guide to the street's restaurants and Elise chose the old small reliable subterranean bistro. Eric looked out the window and saw a crack in the wall called Little Tokyo.

The place was empty.

"You're wearing a cashmere sweater."

"Yes I am."

"It's beige."

"Yes."

"And that's your hand-beaded skirt."

"Yes it is."

"I'm noticing. How was the play?"

"I left at intermission, didn't I?"

"What was it about and who was in it? I'm making conversation."

"I went on impulse. The audience was sparse. Five minutes after the curtain went up, I understood why."

The waiter stood by the table. Elise ordered a mixed green salad, if manageable, and a small bottle of mineral water. Not sparkling, please, but still.

Eric said, "Give me the raw fish with mercury poisoning."

He sat facing the street. Danko stood just outside the door, unaccompanied by the female.

"Where is your jacket?"

"Where is my jacket."

"You were wearing a suit jacket earlier. Where is your jacket?"

"Lost in the scuffle, I guess. You saw the car. We were under attack by anarchists. Just two hours ago they were a major global protest. Now, what, forgotten."

"There's something else I wish I could forget."

"That's my peanuts you smell."

"Didn't I see you come out of the hotel just up the street while I was standing outside the theater?"

He was enjoying this. It put her at a disadvantage, playing petty interrogator, and made him feel boyishly inventive and rebellious.

"I could tell you there was an emergency meeting of my staff to deal with the crisis. The nearest conference room was at the hotel. Or I could tell you I had to use the men's room in the lobby. There's a toilet in the car but you don't know this. Or I went to the health club at the hotel to work off the tension of the day. I could tell you I spent an hour on a treadmill. Then I went for a swim if there's a swimming pool. Or I went up to the roof to watch the lightning flash. I love it when the rain has that wavering quality it rarely has these days. It's that whiplash sort of quality, where the rain undulates above the rooftops. Or the car's liquor cabinet was unaccountably empty and I went in to have a drink. I could tell you I went in to have a drink, in the bar off the lobby, where the peanuts are always fresh."

The waiter said, "Enjoy."

She looked at her salad. Then she began to eat it. She dug right in, treating it as food and not some extrusion of matter that science could not explain.

"Is that the hotel you wanted to take me to?"

"We don't need a hotel. We'll do it in the ladies' room. We'll go to the alley out back and rattle the garbage cans. Look. I'm trying to make contact in the most ordinary ways. To see and hear. To notice your mood, your clothes. This is important. Are your stockings on straight? I understand this at some level. How people look. What people wear."

"How they smell," she said. "Do you mind my saying that? Am I being too wifely? I'll tell you what the problem is. I don't know how to be indifferent. I can't master this. And it makes me susceptible to pain. In other words it hurts."

"This is good. We're like people talking. Isn't this how they talk?"

"How would I know?"

He swallowed his sake. There was a long pause.

He said, "My prostate is asymmetrical."

She sat back and thought, looking at him with some concern.

"What does that mean?"

119

He said, "I don't know."

There was a palpable adjustment, a shared disquiet and sensitivity.

"You have to see a doctor."

"I just saw a doctor. I see a doctor every day."

The room, the street were completely still and they were whispering now. He didn't think they'd ever felt so close.

"You just saw a doctor."

"That's how I know."

They thought about this. With the moment growing solemn, something faintly humorous passed between them. Maybe there is humor in certain parts of the body even as their dysfunction slowly kills you, loved ones gathered at the bed, above the soiled sheets, others in the foyer smoking.

"Look. I married you for your beauty but you don't have to be beautiful. I married you for your money in a way, the history of it, piling up over generations, through world wars. This is not something I need but a little history is nice. The family retainers. The vintage cellars. Little intimate wine tastings. Spitting merlot together. This is stupid but nice. The estate-bottled wines. The statuary in the Renaissance garden, beneath the hilltop villa, among the lemon groves. But you don't have to be rich."

"I just have to be indifferent."

She began to cry. He'd never seen her cry and felt a little helpless. He put out a hand. It remained there, extended, between them.

"You wore a turban at our wedding."

"Yes."

"My mother loved that," she said.

"Yes. But I'm feeling a change. I'm making a change. Did you look at the menu? They have green tea ice cream. This is something you might like. People change. I know what's important now."

"That's such a boring thing to say. Please."

"I know what's important now."

"All right. But note the skeptical tone," she said. "What's important now?"

"To be aware of what's around me. To understand another person's situation, another person's feelings. To know, in short, what's important. I thought you had to be beautiful. But this isn't true anymore. It was true earlier in the day. But nothing that was true then is true now."

"Which means, I take it, that you don't think I'm beautiful."

"Why do you have to be beautiful?"

"Why do you have to be rich, famous, brainy, powerful and feared?"

His hand was still suspended in the air between them. He took her water bottle and drank what remained. Then he told her that Packer Capital's portfolio had been reduced to near nothingness in the course of the day and that his personal fortune in the tens of billions was in ruinous convergence with this fact. He also told her that someone out there in the rainswept night had made a credible threat on his life. Then he watched her absorb the news.

121

He said, "You're eating. That's good."

But she wasn't eating. She was absorbing the news, sitting in a white silence, fork poised. He wanted to take her out in the alley and have sex with her. Beyond that, what? He did not know. He could not imagine. But then he never could. It made sense to him that his immediate and extended futures would be compressed into whatever events might constitute the next few hours, or minutes, or less. These were the only terms of life expectancy he'd ever recognized as real.

"It's okay. It's fine," he said. "It makes me feel free in a way I've never known."

"That's so awful. Don't say things like that. Free to do what? Go broke and die? Listen to me. I'll help you financially. I'll truly do what I can do to help. You can reestablish yourself, at your pace, in your way. Tell me what you need. I promise I'll help. But as a couple, as a marriage, I think we're done, aren't we? You speak of being free. This is your lucky day."

He'd left his wallet in the jacket in the hotel room. She took the check and began to cry again. She cried through tea with lemon and then they walked to the door together, in close embrace, her head resting on his shoulder.

He found his cigar smoldering in an ashtray on the liquor cabinet and he fired it up again. The aroma gave him a sense of robust health. He smelled well-being, long life, even placid fatherhood, somewhere, in the burning leaf.

There was another theater across the street, near the

desolate end of the block, the Biltmore, and he saw scaffolding out front and construction rubble in a dumpster nearby. A restoration project was underway and the front doors were bolted but there were people slipping into the stage entrance, young men and women in slinky pairs and clusters, and he heard random noise, or industrial sounds, or music in massive throbs and blots coming from deep inside the building.

He knew he was going in. But first he had to lose more money.

The crystal on his wristwatch was also a screen. When he activated the online function, the other features receded. It took him a moment to decode a series of encrypted signatures. This is how he used to hack into corporate systems, testing their security for a fee. He did it this time to examine the bank, brokerage and offshore accounts of Elise Shifrin and then to impersonate her algorithmically and transfer the money in these accounts to Packer Capital, where he opened a new account for her, more or less instantaneously, by thumbnailing some numbers on the tiny keypad that was set around the bezel of the watch. Then he went about losing the money, spreading it systematically in the smoke of rumbling markets. He did this to make certain he could not accept her offer of financial help. The gesture had touched him but it was necessary to resist, of course, or die in his soul. But this wasn't the only reason to piss away her birthright. He was making a gesture of his own, a sign of ironic final binding. Let it all come down. Let them see each other pure and lorn. This was the individual's revenge on the mythical couple.

How much was she worth?

The number surprised him. The total in U.S. dollars was seven hundred and thirty-five million. The number seemed puny, a lottery jackpot shared by seventeen postal workers. The words sounded puny and tinny and he tried to be ashamed on her behalf. But it was all air anyway. It was air that flows from the mouth when words are spoken. It was lines of code that interact in simulated space.

Let them see each other clean, in killing light.

Danko preceded him to the stage door. A bouncer was stationed there, immense, steroidal, wearing thumb rings set with jewelled skulls. Danko spoke to him, opening his jacket to reveal the weapon holstered there, an evidence of credentials, and the man gave directions. Eric followed his bodyguard down a plastery damp passageway, up a steep flight of narrow metal stairs and onto a catwalk above the fly space.

He looked down on a gutted theater pounding with electronic sound. Bodies were packed tight through the orchestra and loges and there were dancers in the debris of the second balcony, not torn down yet, and they spread down the stairs and into the lobby, bodies in cyclonic dance, and on the stage and in the pit more tossing bodies in a wash of achromatic light.

A bedsheet banner, hand-lettered, dangled from the balcony.

The music was cold and repetitive, computer-looped into long percussive passages with distant tunneling sounds under the pulsebeat.

"This is very crazy. Take over whole theater. What do you think?" Danko said.

"I don't know."

"I don't know either. But I think it is crazy. Looks like drug scene. What do you think?"

"Yes."

"I think it is latest drug. Called novo. Makes pain go away. Look how good they feel."

"Kids."

"They are kids. Exactly. What pain do they feel that they need to take pill? Music, okay, too loud, so what. It is beautiful how they dance. But what pain do they feel too young to buy beer?"

"There's pain enough for everybody now," Eric told him.

It was hard work to talk and listen. Finally they had to look at each other, read lips through the stunning noise. Now that he knew Danko's name, he could see him, partially. This was a man about forty, average size, scarred across the forehead and cheek, with a bent nose and bristled hair cut close. He did not live in his clothes, his turtleneck and blazer, but in a body hammered out of raw experience, things suffered and done to extreme limits.

Music devoured the air around them, issuing from

enormous speakers set among the ruined murals on facing walls. He began to feel an otherworldliness, a strange arrhythmia in the scene. The dancers seemed to be working against the music, moving ever more slowly as the tempo compressed and accelerated. They opened their mouths and rolled their heads. All the boys had ovoid heads, the girls were a cult of starvelings. The light source was in the tech level above the balcony, radiating long cool waves of banded gray. To someone watching from above, light fell upon the ravers with a certain clemency of effect, a visual counterstroke to the ominous sound. There was a remote track under the music that resembled a female voice but wasn't. It spoke and moaned. It said things that seemed to make sense but didn't. He listened to it speak outside the range of any language ever humanly employed and he began to miss it when it stopped.

"I don't believe I am here," Danko said.

He looked at Eric and smiled at the idea of being here, among American teenagers in stylized riot, with music that took you over, replacing your skin and brain with digital tissue. There was something infectious in the air. It wasn't the music and lights alone that drew you in, the spectacle of massed dance in a theater stripped of seats and paint and history. Eric thought it might be the drug as well, the novo, spreading its effect from those who took it to those who did not. You caught what they had. First you were apart and watching and then you were in, and with, and of the crowd, and then you were the crowd, densely assembled and dancing as one.

126

They were weightless down there. He thought the drug was probably dissociative, separating mind from body. They were a blank crowd, outside worry and pain, drawn to the glassy repetition. All the menace of electronica was in repetition itself. This was their music, loud, bland, bloodless and controlled, and he was beginning to like it.

But he felt old, watching them dance. An era had come and gone without him. They melted into each other so they wouldn't shrivel up as individuals. The noise was nearly unbearable, taking root in his hair and teeth. He was seeing and hearing too much. But this was his only defense against the spreading mental state. Never having touched or tasted the drug, not even having seen it, he felt a little less himself, a little more the others, down there, raving.

"You tell me when we leave. I take you out."

"Where is he?"

"At the entrance. Torval? He watches at the entrance."

"Have you killed people?"

"What do you think? Like lunch," he said.

They were in a trance state now, dancing in slowest motion. The music took a turn toward dirge, with lyrical keyboard flourishes bridging every segment of regret. It was the last techno-rave, the end of whatever it was the end of.

Danko led him down the long stairway and through the passage. There were dressing rooms with ravers inside, sitting and lying everywhere, slumped against each other. He stood in a doorway and watched. They could not speak or walk. One of them licked another's face, the only movement in the room. Even as his self-awareness grew weaker, he could see who they were in their chemical delirium and it was tender and moving, to know them in their frailty, their wistfulness of being, because kids is all they were, trying not to scatter in the air.

He'd walked nearly to the stage door when he realized Danko was not with him. This he understood. The man was back there somewhere dancing, beyond the reach of his wars and corpses, his mind snipers firing at first light.

He went stride for stride with Torval to the car. The rain had stopped. This was good. This was clearly what it should have done. The street carried a shimmer of sodium lamps and a mood of slowly unfolding suspense.

"Where is he?"

"Decided to stay inside," Eric said.

"Good. We don't need him."

"Where is she?"

"Sent her home."

"Good."

"Good," Torval said. "It's looking good."

There was someone camped in the limo. She sat tilted on the banquette, nodding off, all plastic and rags, and Torval rousted her out. She did a little dance of twisting free and remained there in aggregate, a standing heap of clothes, bundled possessions and sandwich bags for alms looped over her belt.

"I need a gypsy. Anybody here read palms?"

One of those unused voices that sound outside the world.

"What about feet?" she said. "Read my feet."

He searched his pockets for money, feeling a little foolish, a little chagrined, having made and lost sums that could colonize a planet, but the woman was moving up the street on shoes with flapping soles and there were no bills or coins in any case to find inside his pants, or documents of any kind.

The car crossed Eighth Avenue, out of the theater district, out of the row of supper clubs and lounges, beyond the retail atriums now, beyond the airline offices and auto showrooms and into the local, the mixed, the mostly unnoticed blocks of dry cleaner and schoolyard, just an inkling here of the old brawl, the old seethe and heat of Hell's Kitchen, the rake of fire escapes on old brick buildings.

Traffic was scant but the car kept to the daylong draggy pace. This is because Eric was in his seat talking through the open window to Torval, who walked alongside the automobile.

"What do we know?"

"We know it's not a group. It's not an organized terror cell or international kidnappers with ransom demands."

"It's an individual. Do we care?"

"We don't have a name. But we have a phone call. The complex is analyzing voice data. They've made certain assessments. And they're projecting a course of action on the part of the individual."

"Why can't I work up any curiosity on the subject?"

"Because it doesn't matter," Torval said. "Whoever it is, that's who it is."

Eric agreed with this, whatever it meant. They moved down the street between rows of garbage cans set out for collection and past the gaunt hotel and the synagogue for actors. There was muddy water in the street, deepening as they proceeded, three, four inches now, the residue of the water-main break earlier in the day. Workers in day-glo vests and high boots were still in the area, under floodlights, and Torval high-stepped through generations of muck, making a splash with each bitter stride until the river diminished to an inch of standing water.

There were police barricades just ahead, blocking access to Ninth Avenue. At first Torval believed this was related to the flooded streets. But there were no clean-up crews on the other side of the avenue. Then he thought the president's motorcade was on the way downtown to some official function after finally shaking free of midtown traffic. But there was music in the distance and people beginning to gather, too many, too young, with headsets attached, to account for a presidential drive-by. Finally he talked to one of the cops at the barricades.

There was a funeral on the way.

Eric got out of the car and stood near the bicycle shop on the corner, with Torval planted nearby. An enormous man approached through the gathering crowd, broad, meaty, solemn, wearing pale linen slacks and a black leather shirt, sleeveless, with platinum accessories here and there. It was Kozmo Thomas, who managed a dozen rappers and had once owned a stable of racehorses in partnership with Eric.

They did the handclasp and half hug.

"Why are we here?"

"You ain't heard?"

Eric said, "What?"

Kozmo batted himself in the chest, reverently.

"Brutha Fez."

"What?"

"Dead."

"No. What. Can't be."

"Dead. Died. Early today."

"I don't know this?"

"Funeral's been in progress all day. The family wants to give the city a chance to pay respect. The record label wants an exploitation event. Big and loud. Street to street. Right through the night."

"I don't know this? How can this be? I love his music. I have his music in my elevator. I know the man."

He knew the man. The sadness, the plangency of this remark was echoed in the music itself, the *qawwali* model of devotional rhythms and improvisations, over a thousand years old, growing louder now as the funeral cortege came down the avenue, which had been cleared of extraneous traffic and parked cars.

"What, they shot him?"

First the squad of motorcycles, city police in wedge formation. Two private security vans followed, flanking a police cruiser. It was so completely clear, another dead rapper, the protocol of the rap star who goes down humming in a spatter of gunshots after he fails to pay feudal tribute in the form of respect or money or women to some skittish individual. This was the day, was it not, for influential men to come to sudden messy ends.

Kozmo was looking askance.

"Fez been having cardiac problems for years. Since high school. Been seeing specialists, been seeing faith healers. Heart just wore out. This ain't a thug down some alley. The man never been breathalyzed, barely, since he was seventeen."

Then came the flower cars, ten of them, banked with white roses rippling in the breeze. The hearse came next, an open car with Fez lying in state at the rear in a coffin angled upward to make the body visible, asphodels everywhere, fleshy pink, the flowers of Hades, where souls of the dead come to find meadowy rest.

The dead man's amplified voice sounded from farther back in the procession, singing in slow hypnotic syncopation, accompanied by harmonium and hand drums.

"Hope you're not disappointed."

"Disappointed."

"That our man here wasn't shot. Hope he didn't let you down. Natural causes. That's a letdown."

Kozmo jabbed a thumb back over his shoulder.

"What happened to your stretch? Letting a fine machine degrade in public. That's a scandal, man."

"Everything's a scandal. Dying's a scandal. But we all do it."

"I'm hearing voices in the night. Because I know it can't be you that's saying this."

Scores of women walked alongside the limousines, in headscarves and djellabas, hands stained with henna, and barefoot, and wailing. Kozmo struck his chest again and so did Eric. He thought his friend was impressive in repose, wearing a full beard and a white silk caftan with hood folded back and the iconic red fez on his head, stylishly tilted, and how affecting it was for the man to be lying in the spiral of his own vocal adaptations of ancient Sufi music, rapping in Punjabi and Urdu and in the black-swagger English of the street.

> Gettin' shot is easy
> Tried it seven times
> Now I'm just a solo poet
> Workin' on my rhymes

The crowd was large and hushed, deepening along the sidewalks, and people in nightclothes watched from tenement windows. Four of Fez's personal bodyguards accompanied the hearse, slow-marching, one off each point of the car. They were in Western dress, dark suits and ties, polished oxfords, with combat shotguns held at port arms.

Eric liked that. Bodyguards even in death. Eric thought *yes*.

Then came the breakdancers, in pressed jeans and sneakers, here to affirm the history of the deceased, born Raymond Gathers in the Bronx, once a breaker of some fame. These were his contemporaries, six men ranged across the six lanes of the avenue, in their mid-thirties now, back in the streets after all these years to do their windmills and reels, their impossible axial headspins.

"Ask me do I love this shit," said Kozmo.

But the energy and dazzle brought something melancholy to the crowd, more regret than excitation. Even the younger people seemed subdued, over-respectful, as the breakers wheeled on their elbows and flared their bodies parallel to the ground, running in horizontal frenzy.

Grief should be powerful, Eric thought. But the crowd was still learning how to mourn a singular rapper such as Fez, who mixed languages, tempos and themes.

Only Kozmo was alive and popping.

"Me being big as I am, and a retro-nigger, I have to love what I'm seeing. Because this is something I could never dream of doing in my thinnest day on earth."

Yes, they spun on their heads, bodies upright and legs spread slightly, and one of the breakers had his hands cuffed behind his back. Eric thought there was something mystical about this, well beyond the scan of human encompassment, the half-crazed passion of a desert saint. How lost to the world he must be, here in the grease and tar of Ninth Avenue.

Family and friends came next, in thirty-six white stretch limousines, three abreast, with the mayor and police commissioner in sober profile, and a dozen members of Congress, and the mothers of unarmed blacks shot by police, and fellow rappers in the middle phalanx, and there were

134

media executives, foreign dignitaries, faces from film and TV, and mingled throughout were figures of world religion in their robes, cowls, kimonos, sandals and soutanes.

Four news choppers passed overhead.

"He liked having his clergy nearby," Kozmo said. "He showed up in my office once with an imam and two white boys from Utah in suits. He was always excusing himself so he could pray."

"He lived in a minaret for a while, in Los Angeles."

"I heard that."

"I went to visit once. He built it next to his house and then moved out of the house and into the minaret."

The dead man's voice was louder now as the sound truck approached. His best songs were sensational and even the ones that were not good were good.

Behind his voice the handclapping of the chorus became intense, driving Fez into improvised rhythms that sounded reckless and unsustainable. There were great howls of devotion, whoops and street shouts. The clapping spread from the recorded track to the people in the limos and the crowd on the sidewalks and it brought a clear emotion to the night, a joy of intoxicating wholeness, he and they, the dead and provisionally living.

A line of elderly Catholic nuns in full habit recited the rosary, teachers from the grade school he'd attended.

His voice was going ever faster, in Urdu, then slurry English, and it was pierced by the shrill cries of a female member of the chorus. There was rapture in this, fierce elation, and something else that was inexpressible, drop-

135

ping off the edge, all meaning exhausted until nothing was left but charismatic speech, words sprawling over themselves, without drums or handclaps or the woman's pitched cries.

The voice fell into silence finally. People thought the event was over now. They were shaking and drained. Eric's delight in going broke seemed blessed and authenticated here. He'd been emptied of everything but a sense of surpassing stillness, a fatedness that felt disinterested and free.

Then he thought about his own funeral. He felt unworthy and pathetic. Never mind the bodyguards, four versus three. What set of elements might be configured that could possibly match what was happening here? Who would come to see him laid out? (An embalmed term in search of a matching cadaver.) Men he'd crushed, to nourish their rancor. Those he'd presumed to be wallpaper, to stand over him and gloat. He would be the powdered body in the mummy case, the one they'd all lived long enough to mock.

It was dispiriting, then, to think about this collection of mourners. Here was a spectacle he could clearly not command. And the funeral wasn't over yet.

Because here came the dervishes, turning to the faint call of a single flute. They were lean men in tunics and long flared skirts, with topaz caps, brimless, cylindrical, tall. They spun, they turned slowly with arms wide and heads titled slightly.

Now the voice of Brutha Fez, hoarse and unaccompanied, moving slowly through a plainsong rap Eric hadn't heard before.

> *Kid used to think he was wise to the system*
> *Prince of the street always do things his way*
> *But he had a case of conventional wisdom*
> *Never say nothing the others don't say*

The young breakdancer who invites the peril of the street, his arrests and beatings, the panhandling dances on subway platforms, his shame in verse after verse, women shiny in tights, unaffordable, and then the moment of disclosure.

> *Thread of dawn that wakes the East*
> *To the cry of souls unfolding*

His embrace of Sufi tradition, the struggle to become another kind of panhandler, a beggar for rhymes, singing his anti-matter rap (as he called it) and learning languages and customs that seemed natural to him, not sealed in mystery and foreignness, a blessing embedded in the skin.

> *O God O Man living high at last*
> *Sucking the titmilk of prayer and fast*

Wealth, honor in a hundred countries, armored cars and bodyguards, shiny women, yes, again, everywhere now, another blessing of the flesh, women veiled and blue-jeaned, clutching the bedposts, painted women and plain, and he sang a little sorrowfully of this and of the voice in a visionary dream that spoke to him of a failing heart.

> *Man gave me the news in a slanted room*
> *And it felt like a sliver of icy truth*
> *Felt my sad-ass soul flying out of my mouth*
> *My gold tooth splitting down to the root*

There were twenty dervishes in the street and they were the archetype, perhaps, the early and sacred model, maybe, of the posse of breakdancers, only rightside-up. And Fez's final words could find no beauty in dying young.

> *Let me be who I was*
> *Unrhymed fool*
> *That's lost but living*

Now music filled the night, ouds, flutes, cymbals and drums, and the dancers whirled, counterclockwise, faster with every turn. They were spinning out of their bodies, he thought, toward the end of all possessions.

The chorus chanting vigorously now.

Because whirl is all. Whirl is the drama of shedding everything. Because they are spinning into communal grace, he thought. And because someone is dead tonight and only whirl can appease their grief.

He believed these things. He tried to imagine a kind

of fleshlessness. He thought of the whirlers deliquescing, resolving into fluid states, into spinning liquid, rings of water and fog that eventually disappear in air.

He began to weep as the follow-up security detail went past, a police van and several unmarked cars. He wept violently. He pummeled himself, crossing his arms and beating his fists on his chest. The press buses came next, three of them, and unofficial mourners on foot, many resembling pilgrims, all races and styles of belief and manner of dress, and he rocked and wept as mourners in cars went by, an improvised continuum, eighty, ninety cars in slack ranks.

He wept for Fez and everyone here and for himself of course, yielding completely to enormous body sobs. Others were weeping nearby. There was a wave of breast-beating and flailing. Then Kozmo wrapped an arm around him and drew him in. It did not seem strange that this was happening. When people die, you weep. The greater the figure, the more widespread the lamentation. People pulled their hair, wailing the dead man's name. Eric slowly grew still. In the leather and flesh of Kozmo's enveloping bulk, he felt the beginnings of thoughtful acceptance.

There was one thing more he wanted from this funeral. He wanted to see the hearse pass by again, the body tilted for viewing, a digital corpse, a loop, a replication. It did not seem right that the hearse had come and gone. He wanted it to reappear at intervals, proud body open to the night, to replenish the sorrow and wonder of the crowd.

*   *   *

139

He was tired of looking at screens. Plasma screens were not flat enough. They used to seem flat, now they did not. He watched the president of the World Bank address a chamber of tense economists. He thought the image could be crisper. Then the president of the United States spoke from his limo in English and Finnish. He knew a little Finnish. Eric hated him for that. He knew they would figure it out eventually, how he'd made it happen, one man, bereaved and tired now. He coded the screens into their hatches and cabinets, restoring the interior of the car to its natural grandness of scale, with sightlines unobstructed and his body isolated in space, and he felt a sneeze begin to develop in his immune system.

The streets emptied fast, barricades loaded into trucks and hauled away. The car moved forward now, with Torval seated up front.

He sneezed and then felt a sense of incompleteness. He realized that he always sneezed twice, or so it seemed in retrospect. He waited and it came, rewardingly, the second sneeze.

What causes people to sneeze? A protective reflex of the nasal mucous membranes, to expel invasive materials.

The street was dead. The car moved past the Spanish church and the cluster of scaffolded brownstones. He poured a brandy and felt hungry again.

There was a restaurant ahead, on the south side of the street. He saw it was Ethiopian and imagined a chunk of spongy brown bread dragged through lentil stew. He imagined yebeg wat in berber sauce. It was too late for the place to be open but there was a dim light back toward the kitchen and he had the driver stop the car.

He wanted yebeg wat. He wanted to say it, smell it and eat it.

What happened next happened fast. He stepped onto the sidewalk and a man approached running and struck him. He raised an arm in defense, Eric did, too late, and threw a blind punch, maybe grazing the man on the head or shoulder. He felt the sludge, the sort of mush of blood and matter on his face. He could not see. His eyes were coated with the stuff but he heard Torval nearby, their rustles and grunts as the two men skirmished.

He took a handkerchief out of his pocket and stood on the curbstone wiping his face, cautiously, in the event an eyeball had been dislodged. He was able to see that Torval had the man bent over the trunk of the limo, forearm locked behind his head.

"Subject reduced," Torval said into his lapel.

Eric smelled and tasted something. First there was the handkerchief, soured by his own secretions of the testes and seminal vesicles and various other glands, collected earlier in the day when he'd used the square of cloth to clean himself after one or another expulsion of fluid. But he was confused about the taste on his tongue.

The man, the subject was saying something and there were radiant bursts, as of muzzle flash nearby, but without ensuing reports. Torval yanked the man off the rear of the car and splayed him toward Eric, then snapped his head back smartly.

"I am after you long time. Son of bitch," he said. "I glop you good."

Now Eric saw three photographers off to the right and a man shooting video from his knees. Their car sat with doors flung open.

"Today you are crèmed by the master," he said. "This is my mission worldwide. To sabotage power and wealth."

He began to understand. This was André Petrescu, the pastry assassin, a man who stalked corporate directors, military commanders, soccer stars and politicians. He hit them in the face with pies. He blindsided heads of state under house arrest. He ambushed war criminals and the judges who sentenced them.

"I am three years waiting for this. Fresh baked only. I pass up president of the United States to make this strike. I crème him any time. You are major statement, I tell you this. Very hard to zero in."

He was a small guy with hair dyed glossy blond, in a Disney World T-shirt. Eric caught the note of admiration in his voice. Carefully he kicked him in the nuts, watching him spaz and crumple in Torval's grip. When the flash units lit up, he attacked the photographers, landing a number of punches, feeling better with each one. The three backpedaling men stumbled into a row of garbage cans, then scuttled up the street. The videographer fled in the car.

He walked back toward the limo, ladling whipped cream off his face and eating it, snowy topping with a trace of

142

lemon in the taste. He and Torval were bonded now by violence and exchanged a look of respect and esteem.

Petrescu was in pain.

"You lack of humor, Mr. Packer."

Eric gave him a forearm shiver, bouncing him off Torval's chest. It took the man a while to speak.

"You are living up to reputation, okay. But I am kicked and beaten by security so many times I am walking dead. They make me to wear a radio collar when I am in England, to safe the queen. Track me like rare crane. But believe one thing please. I crèmed Fidel three times in six days when he is in Bucharest last year. I am action painter of crème pies. I drop from a tree on Michael Jordan one time. This is famous Flying Pie. It is museum quality video for the ages. I quiche Sultan of fucking Brunei in his bath. They put me in black hole until I am screaming from my eyes."

They watched him stumble away. The restaurant was locked and empty and they stood in the hush of the moment. Eric had whipped cream in his hair and ears. His clothes were streaked with cream and dashes of lemon pie. He could feel a cut on his forehead from a camera one of the men had wielded in self-defense. He needed to take a leak.

He felt great. He held his clenched fist in the other hand. It felt great, it stung, it was quick and hot. His body whispered to him. It hummed with the action, the charge at the photographers, the punches he'd thrown, the bloodsurge, the heartbeat, the great strewn beauty of garbage cans toppling.

He was brass-balled again.

He found his sunglasses in the champagne well and put them in his shirt pocket. There was a sound outside, a bouncing ball. He was about to give the driver the signal to move when he heard the sporadic heavy bounce of a basketball, unmistakable. He got out of the car and crossed to the north side of the street, where a playground was located. He looked through two fences and saw a couple of kids crouched and growling, going one-on-one.

The first gate was locked. He climbed the fence of spiked iron palings without hesitation. The second gate was also locked. He climbed the chain-link fence, which was twice as high. He went up and over and Torval followed, fence to fence, wordlessly.

They went to the far end of the park and watched the kids go at it, playing in shadow and murk.

"You play?"

"Some. Not really my game," Torval said. "Rugby. That was my game. You play?"

"Some. I liked the action in the paint. I pump iron now."

"Of course you understand. There's still someone tracking you."

"There's still someone out there."

"This was a petty incursion. The whipped cream. Technically irrelevant."

"I understand. I realize. Of course."

144

They were intense, these kids, hand-slapping and banging for rebounds, making throaty sounds.

"Next time no pies and cakes."

"Dessert is over."

"He's out there and he's armed."

"He's armed and you're armed."

"This is true."

"You will have to draw your weapon."

"This is true," Torval said.

"Let me see the thing."

"Let you see the thing. Okay. Why not? You paid for it."

The two men made little snuffling sounds, insipid nasal laughter.

Torval removed the weapon from his jacket and handed it over, a handsome piece of equipment, silver and black, four-and-a-half-inch barrel, walnut stock.

"Manufactured in the Czech Republic."

"Nice."

"Smart too. Scary smart."

"Voice recognition."

"That's right," Torval said.

"You what. You speak and it knows your voice."

"That's right. The mechanism doesn't activate unless the voiceprint matches the stored data. Only my voice matches."

"Do you have to speak Czech before it fires?"

Torval smiled broadly. It was the first time Eric had seen him smile. With his free hand he took the sunglasses out of his shirt pocket and shook the temples loose.

"But the voice is only half the operation," Torval said, then paused invitingly.

"You're saying there's a code as well."

"A preprogrammed spoken code."

Eric put on the glasses.

"What is it?"

Torval smiled privately this time, then raised his eyes to Eric, who leveled the weapon now.

"Nancy Babich."

He shot the man. A small white terror of disbelief flickered in Torval's eye. He fired once and the man went down. All authority drained out of him. He looked foolish and confused.

The basketball stopped bouncing twenty yards away.

He had mass but no flow. This was clear as he lay there dying. He had discipline and a sense of pace, okay, but no true fluency of movement.

Eric glanced at the kids, who stood motionless watching. The ball was on the ground and slowly rolling. He gave them a casual hand signal indicating they ought to continue their game. Nothing so meaningful had happened that they were required to stop playing.

He tossed the weapon in the bushes and walked toward the chain-link fence.

There were no windows flying open or concerned voices calling. The weapon was not equipped with a sound suppressor but there'd been only one shot and maybe people needed to hear three, four, more to rouse them from sleep or television. This was one of the routine ephemera of the

146

night, no different from cats at sex or a backfiring car. Even if you know it's not a backfiring car, because it never is, you don't feel a prod to conscience unless the apparent gunfire is repeated and there are sounds of running men. In the dense stir of the neighborhood, living so close to street level, with noises all the time and the dead-ass drift of your personal urban anomie, you can't be expected to react to an isolated bang.

Too, the shot was less annoying than the basketball game. If the effect of the shot was to end the game, be grateful for moonlit favors.

He paused imperceptibly, thinking he ought to go back for the weapon.

He'd tossed the weapon in the bushes because he wanted whatever would happen to happen. Guns were small practical things. He wanted to trust the power of pre-determined events. The act was done, the gun should go.

He climbed the chain-link fence, tearing his pants at the pocket.

He'd tossed the weapon rashly but how fantastic it had felt. Lose the man, shed the gun. Too late now to reconsider.

He dropped to the ground and advanced to the iron fence.

He didn't wonder who Nancy Babich was and he didn't think that Torval's choice of code humanized the man or required delayed regret. Torval was his enemy, a threat to his self-regard. When you pay a man to keep you alive, he gains a psychic edge. It was a function of the credible

147

threat and the loss of his company and personal fortune that Eric could express himself this way. Torval's passing cleared the night for deeper confrontation.

He scaled the iron fence and walked to the car. A man from the century past played a saxophone on the corner.

The Confessions
of Benno Levin

MORNING

I am living offline now. I am all bared down. I am writing this at my iron desk, which I pushed along the sidewalk and into this building. I have my exercise bike where I real-pedal with one foot, simulate with the other.

I am planning to make a public act of my life through these pages I will write. This will be a spiritual autobiography that runs to thousands of pages and the core of the work will be either I track him down and shoot him or do not, writing longhand in pencil.

When I was employed I kept small accounts at five major banks. The names of major banks are breathtaking in the mind and there are branches all over town. I used to go to different banks or to branches of the same bank. I had episodes where I went from branch to branch well into the night, moving money between accounts or just check-ing my balances. I entered codes and examined numbers. The machine takes us through the steps. The machine says, Is this correct? It teaches us to think in logic blocks.

I was briefly married to a disabled woman with a child. I used to look at her child, who was barely out of infancy, and think I'd fallen down a hole.

I was teaching and lecturing then. Lecturing is not the word. I dart from subject to subject in my mind. I don't want to do the type of writing where I recite biography, parentage and education. I want to rise up from the words on the page and do something, hurt someone. It is in me to hurt someone and I haven't always known this. The act and depth of writing will tell me if I'm capable.

I frankly want your sympathy. I spend my bare cash every day on bottled water. This is for drinking and bathing. I have my toilet arrangements that I made, my take-out places that I patronize and my water needs in a building without water, heat or lights, except what I provide.

It's hard for me to speak directly to people. I used to try to tell the truth. But it's hard not to lie. I lie to people because this is my language, how I talk. It's the temperature inside the head of who I am. I don't aim remarks at the person I'm speaking to but try to miss him, or glance a remark so to speak off his shoulder.

After a time I began to take satisfaction in this. It was never in me to mean what I said. Every unnecessary lie was another way to build a person. I see this clearly now. No one could help me but myself.

I watched the live video feed from his website all the time. I watched for hours and realistically days. What he said to people, how he turned so sharply in his chair. He thought chairs were largely stupid and demeaning. How he swam when he swam, ate meals, played cards on camera. The way he shuffled the cards. Even though I worked in the same headquarters I waited out on the street to see him leave. I wanted to pinpoint him in my mind. It was important to know where he was, even for a moment. It put my world in order.

They were not lies anyway. They were not falsehoods, most of them, but simple deflections off the listener's body, his or her shoulders, or they were total misses.

To speak directly to a person was unbearable. But in these pages I am going to write my way into truth. Trust me. They demoted me to lesser currencies. I write to slow down my mind but sometimes there is leakage.

Now I bank at one location only because I am dwindling down financially to nothing. It's a small bank with one machine inside, one in the street set into the wall. I use the street machine because the guard will not let me in the bank.

I could tell him I have an account and prove it. But the bank is marble and glass and armed guards. And I accept this. I could tell him I need to check Recent Activity, even though there is none. But I am willing to do my trans-actions outside, at the machine in the wall.

I am ashamed every day, and more ashamed the next. But I will spend the rest of my life in this living space writ-

ing these notes, this journal, recording my acts and reflec-
tions, finding some honor, some worth at the bottom of
things. I want ten thousand pages that will stop the world.

Allow me to speak. I'm susceptible to global strains of
illness. I have occasions of *susto*, which is soul loss, more
or less, from the Caribbean, which I contracted originally
on the Internet some time before my wife took her child
and left, carried down the stairs by her illegal immigrant
brothers.

On the one hand it's all a figment and a myth. On the
other hand I'm susceptible. This work will include descrip-
tions of my symptoms.

He is always ahead, thinking past what is new, and I'm
tempted to admire this, always arguing with things that
you and I consider great and trusty additions to our lives.
Things wear out impatiently in his hands. I know him in
my mind. He wants to be one civilization ahead of this
one.

I used to keep a roll of bills wrapped in a blue rubber-
band that was stamped California Asparagus. That money
is in circulation now, hand to hand, unsanitized. I have a
stationary bike that I found one night with a missing
pedal.

I advertised clandestinely for a used gun and bought it
subtly and privately when I was online and still employed
but barely, knowing the day was coming, he is erratic, his
work habits are disintegrating, which was visible in their
faces, despite the humor and pathos of owning such a
complicated weapon for a person such as me.

I can see the scornful humor and pity in what I do sometimes. And I can almost enjoy it on the level of being helpless.

My life was not mine anymore. But I didn't want it to be. I watched him knot his tie and knew who he was. His bathroom mirror had a readout telling him his temperature and blood pressure at that moment, his height, weight, heart rate, pulse, pending medication, whole health history from looking at his face, and I was his human sensor, reading his thoughts, knowing the man in his mind.

It tells your height in case you shrink at night, which can happen anabolically.

Cigarettes are not part of the profile of the person you think I am. But I'm a violent smoker. I need what I need very badly. I don't read for pleasure. I don't bathe often because it isn't affordable. I buy my clothes at Value Drugs. You can do this in America, dress yourself from a drugstore head to toe, which I admire quietly. But whatever the sundry facts, I'm not so different from you in your inner life in the sense that we're all uncontrollable.

They carried her down the stairs in her wheelchair with her baby. I was disoriented in my head. Maybe you have seen the spikes on a lying polygraph. This is my wave of thought sometimes, thinking how do I respond to this. I left teaching to make my million. It was the right time and tide to do this. But then I felt derived, sitting at my workstation. I felt inserted there, a person in a situation not of his choosing, even though I'd made the choice to be there, and the closest he ever came was overhearing distance.

I'm ambivalent about killing him. Does this make me less interesting to you, or more?

I'm not one of those trodden bodies you try not to look at when you walk down certain streets. I don't look at them either. I'm knocking down the walls in my living space, a task of many weeks that's nearly done now. I buy my bottled water in the Mexican grocery up the street. There are two clerks or an owner and a clerk and they both say No problem. I say Thank you. No problem.

I used to lick coins as a child. The fluting at the edge of a common coin. The milling it is called. I lick them still, sometimes, but worry about the dirt trapped in the milling.

But to take another person's life? This is the vision of the new day. I am determined finally to act. It is the violent act that makes history and changes everything that came before. But how to imagine the moment? I'm not sure I can reach the point of even doing it mentally, two faceless men with runny colored clothes.

And how will I find him to kill, much less actually aim and shoot? So it is largely academic, this give-and-take.

When I pay with coins I go into small fixations of miscounting and fumbling.

But how do I live if he's not dead? He can be a dead father. I will offer this hope. They can harvest his sperm, then freeze it for fifteen months. After this it's a simple matter to impregnate his widow or a voluntary mother.

Then another person will grow into his form and flesh and I will have something to hate when it is old enough to be a man.

People think about who they are in the stillest hour of the night. I carry this thought, the child's mystery and terror of this thought, I feel this immensity in my soul every second of my life.

I have my iron desk that I hauled up three flights of stairs, with ropes and wedges. I have my pencils that I sharpen with a paring knife.

There are dead stars that still shine because their light is trapped in time. Where do I stand in this light, which does not strictly exist?

4

The limousine was a striking sight under the streetlamp, with a bruised cartoonish quality, a car in a narrative panel, it feels and speaks. The opera lights were on, twelve per side, placed between windows in sets of four. The driver stood at the rear, holding open the door. Eric did not enter immediately. He stopped and looked at the driver. He'd never done this before and it took him a while to see the man.

The man was slim and black, medium height. He had a longish face. He had an eye, the left, that was hard to find beneath the deep sag of the lid. The lower rim of the iris was visible, shut off in a corner. The man had a history, evidently. There were evening streaks in the white of the eye, a sense of blood sun. Things had happened in his life.

Eric liked the idea that a man with a devastated eye drove a car for a living. His car. This made it even better.

He remembered that he needed to urinate. He did it in the car, stooping, and watched the bowl fold back into its housing. He didn't know what happened to the waste. Maybe it was tanked up somewhere in the underside of the automobile or possibly dumped directly in the street, violating a hundred statutes.

The car's fog lamps were glowing. The river was only two blocks away, bearing its daily inventory of chemicals and incidental trash, floatable household objects, the odd body bludgeoned or shot, all ghosting prosaically south to the tip of the island and the seamouth beyond.

The light was red. Only the sparsest traffic moved on the avenue ahead and he sat in the car and realized how curious it was that he was willing to wait, no less than the driver, just because a light was one color and not another. But he wasn't observing the terms of social accord. He was in a patient mood, that's all, and maybe feeling thoughtful, being mortally alone now, with his body-guards gone.

The car crossed Tenth Avenue and went past the first small grocery and then the truck lot lying empty. He saw two cars parked on the sidewalk, shrouded in torn blue tarp. There was a stray dog, there's always a lean gray dog nosing into wadded pages of a newspaper. The garbage cans here were battered metal, not the gentrified rubber products on the streets to the east, and there was garbage in open boxes and a scatter of trash fanning from a super-market cart upended in the street. He felt a silence descend, an absence unrelated to the mood of the street at this hour, and the car passed the second small grocery and he saw the ramparts above the train tracks that ran below street level and the garages and body shops sealed for the night, steel shutters marked with graffiti in Spanish and Arabic.

The barbershop was on the north side of the street and faced a row of old brick tenements. The car stopped and Eric sat there, thinking. He sat for five, six minutes. Then the door croaked open and the driver stood on the sidewalk, looking in.

"We are here," he said finally.

Eric stood on the sidewalk looking at the tenements across the street. He looked at the middle building in a line of five and felt a lonely chill, fourth floor, windows dark and fire escape bare of plants. The building was grim. It was a grim street but people used to live here in loud close company, in railroad flats, and happy as anywhere, he thought, and still did, and still were.

His father had grown up here. There were times when Eric was compelled to come and let the street breathe on him. He wanted to feel it, every rueful nuance of longing. But it wasn't his longing or yearning or sense of the past. He was too young to feel such things, and anyway unsuited, and this had never been his home or street. He was feeling what his father would feel, standing in this place.

The barbershop was closed. He knew it would be closed at this hour. He went to the door and saw that the back room was lighted. It had to be lighted, whatever the hour. He knocked and waited and the old man came moving through the dimness, Anthony Adubato, in his working outfit, a striped white tunic, short-sleeved, with baggy pants and running shoes.

Eric knew what the man would say when he opened the door.

"But how come you're such a stranger lately?"

"Hello, Anthony."

"Long time."

"Long time. I need a haircut."

"You look like what. Get in here so I can look at you."

He flipped the light switch and waited for Eric to sit in the one barber chair that was left. There was a hole in the linoleum where the other chair had been and there was the toy chair for kids, still here, a green roadster with red steering wheel.

"I never seen such ratty hair on a human."

"I woke up this morning and knew it was time."

"You knew where to come."

"I said to myself. I want a haircut."

The man eased the sunglasses off Eric's head and placed them on the shelf under the room-length mirror, checking them first for smudges and dust.

"Maybe you want to eat something first."

"I could eat something."

"There's take-out in the fridgerator that I nibble at it when I get the urge."

He went into the back room and Eric looked around him. Paint was coming off the walls, exposing splotches of pinkish white plaster, and the ceiling was cracked in places. His father had brought him here many years ago, the first time, and maybe the place had been in better shape but not by much.

Anthony stood in the doorway, a small white carton in each hand.

"So you married that woman."

"That's right."

"That her family's got like money unbeknownst. I never thought you'd get married so young. But what do I know? I have chickpeas mashed up and I have eggplant stuffed with rice and nuts."

"Give me the eggplant."

"You got it," Anthony said, but stood where he was, in the doorway.

"He went fast once they found it. He was diagnosed and then he went. It was like he was talking to me one day and gone the next. In my mind that's how it feels. I also have the other eggplant with garlic and lemon all mashed up together if you want to try that instead. He was diagnosed it was January. They found it and told him. But he didn't tell your mother until he had to. By March he was gone. But in my mind it feels like a day or two. Two days tops."

Eric had heard this a number of times and the man used the same words nearly every time, with topical variations. This is what he wanted from Anthony. The same words. The oil company calendar on the wall. The mirror that needed silvering.

"You were four years old."

"Five."

"Exactly. Your mother was the brains of the outfit. That's where you get your mentality. Your mother had the wisdom. He said that himself."

"And you. You're keeping well?"

"You know me, kid. I could tell you I can't complain. But I could definitely complain. The thing is I don't want to."

He leaned into the room, upper body only, the old stubbled head and pale eyes.

"Because there isn't time," he said.

After a pause he went to the shelf in front of Eric and put the cartons down and took two plastic spoons out of his breast pocket.

"Let me think what I have that we could drink. There's water from the tap. I drink water now. And there's a bottle of liqueur that's been here don't ask how long."

He was wary of the word liqueur, Anthony was. All the words he'd spoken were the ones he'd always spoken and would always speak except for this one word, which made him nervous.

"I could drink some of that."

"Good. Because if your father himself walked in here and I offered him tap water, god forbid, he would rip out my last chair."

"And maybe we could ask my driver to come in. My driver's out in the car."

"We could give him the other eggplant."

"Good. That would be nice. Thank you, Anthony."

*   *   *

They were halfway through the meal, sitting and talking, Eric and the driver, and Anthony was standing and talking. He'd found a spoon for the driver and the two of them drank water out of unmatching mugs.

The driver's name was Ibrahim Hamadou and it turned out that he and Anthony had driven taxis in New York, many years apart.

Eric sat in the barber chair watching the driver, who did not take off his jacket or loosen his necktie. He sat in a folding chair, his back to the mirror, and spooned his food sedately.

"I drove a checkered cab. Big and bouncy," Anthony said. "I drove nights. I was young. What could they do to me?"

"Nights are not so good if you have a wife and child. Besides, I can tell you it was crazy enough in the daytime."

"I loved my cab. I went twelve hours nonstop. I stopped only to pee."

"A man is hit one day by another taxi. He comes flying into my taxi," Ibrahim said. "I mean he is flying in the air. Crash against the windscreen. Right there in my face. Blood is everywhere."

"I never left the garage without my Windex," Anthony said.

"I am Acting Secretary of External Affairs in my previous life. I said to him, Get off from there. I cannot drive with your body on my windscreen."

It was the left side of his face that Eric could not stop looking at. Ibrahim's collapsed eye fascinated him in a childlike way, beyond the shame of staring. The eye twisted away from the nose, the brow was straight and tilted upward. A raised seam of scar tissue traversed the lid. But even with the lid nearly shut, there was a sediment stir to be detected in the eyeball, a roil of eggwhite and mottled blood. The eye had a kind of autonomy, a personality of its own, giving the man a splitness, an unsettling alternative self.

"I ate at the wheel," Anthony said, waving his food carton. "I had my sandwiches in tinfoil."

"I ate at the wheel also. I could not afford to stop driving."

"Where did you pee, Ibrahim? I peed under the Manhattan Bridge."

"This is where I peed, exactly."

"I peed in parks and alleys. I peed in a pet cemetery once."

"Night is better in some ways," Ibrahim said. "I am certain of it."

Eric listened distantly, beginning to feel sleepy. He drank his liqueur out of a scarred shot glass. When he finished eating he put the spoon in the carton and set the carton carefully on the arm of the chair. Chairs have arms and legs that ought to be called by other names. He laid his head back and closed his eyes.

"I was here what," Anthony said. "Probably four hours a day, helping my father cut hair. Nights I drove my cab. I loved my cab. I had my little fan that worked on a battery because forget about air-conditioning in that day and age. I had my drinking cup with a magnet that I stuck on the dashboard."

"I had my steering wheel upholstered," Ibrahim said. "Very nice, in zebra. And my daughter with her photograph on the visor."

In time the voices became a single vowel sound and this would be the medium of his escape, a breathy passage out of the long pall of wakefulness that had marked so many nights. He began to fade, to drop away, and felt a question trembling in the dark somewhere.

What can be simpler than falling asleep?

First he heard the sound of chewing. He knew where he was at once. Then he opened his eyes and saw himself in the mirror, the room massing around him. He lingered on the image. The eye was mousing up where the edge of the pie crust had struck him. The camera cut on his forehead was discharging a mulberry scab. There was the foaming head of hair, wild and snarled, impressive in a way, and he nodded at himself, taking it all in, full face, remembering who he was.

The barber and driver were sharing a dessert of finely layered pastry glutted with honey and nuts, each holding a square in the palm of his hand.

Anthony was looking at him but speaking to Ibrahim, or to both of them, speaking to the walls and chairs.

"I gave this guy his first haircut. He wouldn't sit in the car seat. His father tried to jam him in there. He's going no no no no. So I put him right where he's sitting now. His father pinned him down," Anthony said. "I cut his father's hair when he was a kid. Then I cut his hair."

He was speaking to himself, to the man he'd been, scissors in hand, clipping a million heads. He kept looking at Eric, who knew what was coming and waited.

"His father grew up with four brothers and sisters. They lived right across the street there. The five kids, the mother, the father, the grandfather, all in one apartment. Listen to this."

Eric listened.

"Eight people, four rooms, two windows, one toilet. I can hear his father's voice. Four rooms, two with windows. It was a statement he liked to make."

Eric sat in the chair and half-dreamed scenes and wavery faces out of his father's mind, faces levitating in his father's sleep or his momentary reverie or final morphine relief, and there was a kitchen that came and went, enamel-top table, wallpaper stains.

"Two with windows," Anthony said.

He almost asked how long he'd been asleep. But people always ask how long they've been asleep. Instead he told them about the credible threat. He confided in them. It felt good to trust someone. It felt right to expose the matter in this particular place, where elapsed time hangs in the air, suffusing solid objects and men's faces. This is where he felt safe.

It was clear that Ibrahim had not been told. He said, "But where is the chief of security in this situation?"

"I gave him the rest of the night off."

Anthony stood by the cash register, chewing.

"But you have protection, right, in the car."

"Protection."

"Protection. You don't know what that means?"

"I had a gun but threw it away."

Ibrahim said, "But why?"

"I wasn't thinking ahead. I didn't want to make plans or take precautions."

"You know how that sounds?" Anthony said. "How does that sound? I thought you had a reputation. Destroy a man in the blink of an eye. But you sound pretty iffy to me. This is Mike Packer's kid? That had a gun and threw it away? What is that?"

"What is that?" Ibrahim said.

"In this part of town? And you don't have a gun?"

"There are steps you must take to safeguard yourself."

"In this part of town?" Anthony said.

"You cannot walk five meters after dark. You will be careless, they kill you straightaway."

Ibrahim was looking at him. It was a flat stare, distant, without a point of contact.

"You will be reasonable with them, they take a little longer. Tear out your entrails first."

He was looking right through Eric. The voice was mild. The driver was a mild figure in a suit and tie, sitting with cake in his outstretched hand, and his comments were clearly personal, extending beyond this city, these streets, the circumstances under discussion.

167

"What happened to your eye," Anthony said, "that it got all twisted that way?"

"I can see. I can drive. I pass their test."

"Because both my brothers were fight trainers years ago. But I never seen a thing like that."

Ibrahim looked away. He would not submit to the tide of memory and emotion. Maybe he felt an allegiance to his history. It is one thing to speak around an experience, use it as reference and analogy. But to detail the hellish thing itself, to strangers who will nod and forget, this must seem a betrayal of his pain.

"You were beaten and tortured," Eric said. "An army coup. Or the secret police. Or they thought they'd executed you. Fired a shot into your face. Left you for dead. Or the rebels. Overrunning the capital. Seizing government people at random. Slamming rifle butts into faces at random."

He spoke quietly. There was a faint sheen of perspiration on Ibrahim's face. He looked wary and prepared, a disposition he'd learned on some sand plain seven hundred years before he was born.

Anthony took a bite of his dessert. They listened to him chew and talk.

"I loved my cab. I gulped my food. I drove twelve hours straight, night after night. Vacations, forget about."

He was standing by the cash register. Then he reached down and opened the cabinet beneath the shelf and lifted out some hand towels.

"But what did I do for protection?"

168

Eric had seen it before, an old pockmarked revolver lying at the bottom of the drawer.

They talked to him. They bared their teeth and ate. They insisted that he take the gun. He wasn't sure it mattered much. He was afraid the night was over. The threat should have taken material form soon after Torval went down but it hadn't, from that point to this, and he began to think it never would. This was the coldest possible prospect, that no one was out there. It left him in a suspended state, all that was worldly and consequential in blurry ruin behind him but no culminating moment ahead.

The only thing left was the haircut.

Anthony billowed the striped cape. He squirted water on Eric's head. The talk was easy now. He refilled the shot glass with sambuca. Then he scissored the air in preparation, an inch from Eric's ear. The talk was routine barbershop, rent hikes and tunnel traffic. Eric held the glass at chin level, arm indrawn, sipping deliberately.

After a while he threw off the cape. He couldn't sit here anymore. He burst from the chair, knocking back the drink in a whiskey swig.

Anthony looked very small, suddenly, with the rake comb in one hand, clippers in the other.

"But how come?"

"I need to leave. I don't know how come. That's how come."

"But let me do the right side at least. So both sides are equal."

It meant something to Anthony. This was clear, getting the sides to match.

"I'll come back. Take my word. I'll sit and you'll finish."

It was the driver who understood. Ibrahim went to the cabinet and removed the gun. Then he handed it butt-first to Eric, a vein flashing on the back of his hand.

There was something determined in his face, a solemn insistence on one's duty to recognize what is harsh and remorseless in the world, and Eric wanted to respond to the staid grave manner of the man, or risk disappointing him.

He took the gun in hand. It was a nickel-plated piece of junk. But he felt the depth of Ibrahim's experience. He tried to read the man's ravaged eye, the bloodshot strip beneath the hooded lid. He respected the eye. There was a story there, a brooding folklore of time and fate.

Steam came venting from a manhole through a tall blue stack, the most common sight, he thought, but beautiful now, carrying the strangeness, the indecipherability of a thing seen new, steam heaving from the urban earth, nearly apparitional.

The car approached Eleventh Avenue. He rode up front with the driver, asking him to cut off all means of communication with the complex. Ibrahim did this. Then he activated the night-vision display. A series of thermal images appeared on the windshield, lower left, objects beyond the range of headlights. He brightened the shot of dumpsters down by the river, adjusting the projection slightly upward. He activated the microcameras that monitored activity on the perimeter of the automobile. Anyone approaching from any angle could be seen on one of the dashboard screens.

These features seemed playthings to Eric, maybe useful in video art.

"Ibrahim, tell me this."

"Yes."

"These stretch limousines that fill the streets. I've been wondering."

"Yes."

"Where are they parked at night? They need large tracts of space. Out near the airports or somewhere in the Meadowlands. Long Island, New Jersey."

"I will go to New Jersey. The limo stays here."

"Where?"

"Next block. There will be an underground garage. Limos only. I will drop off your car, pick up my car, drive home through the stinking tunnel."

An old industrial loft building stood on the southeast corner, ten stories, blocklike, a late medieval sweatshop and firetrap. There were sealed windows and scaffolding and the sidewalk was boarded off. Ibrahim nosed the car farther right, keeping a distance from closed-off areas. A vehicle pulled out in front of them, a lunch van, unlikely at this hour, abnormal, worth watching.

He'd fitted the gun under his belt, uncomfortably. He remembered that he'd slept. He was alert, eager for action, for resolution. Something had to happen soon, a dispelling of doubt and the emergence of some design, the subject's plan of action, visible and distinct.

Then lights came on, dead ahead, flaring with a crack and whoosh, great carbon-arc floodlights that were set on tripods and rigged to lampposts. A woman in jeans appeared, flagging down the car. The intersection was soaked in vibrant light, the night abruptly alive.

People crisscrossed the streets, calling to each other or speaking into handsets, and teamsters unloaded equipment from long trucks parked on both sides of the avenue. Trailers sat in the gas station across the street. The man in the van ahead lowered the fold-over side, for meals, and it was only now that Eric saw the heavy trolley with movable boom attached, rolling slowly into place. Installed at the high end of the boom was a platform that held a movie camera and a couple of seated men.

The crane wasn't the only thing he'd missed. When he got out of the car and moved to a spot that wasn't blocked by the lunch truck, he saw the elements of the scene in preparation.

There were three hundred naked people sprawled in the street. They filled the intersection, lying in haphazard positions, some bodies draped over others, some leveled, flattened, fetal, with children among them. No one was moving, no one's eyes were open. They were a sight to come upon, a city of stunned flesh, the bareness, the bright lights, so many bodies unprotected and hard to credit in a place of ordinary human transit.

Of course there was a context. Someone was making a

movie. But this was just a frame of reference. The bodies were blunt facts, naked in the street. Their power was their own, independent of whatever circumstance attended the event. But it was a curious power, he thought, because there was something shy and wan in the scene, a little withdrawn. A woman coughed with a head-jerk and a leap of the knee. He did not wonder whether they were meant to be dead or only senseless. He found them sad and daring both, and more naked than ever in their lives.

Technicians weaved through the group with light meters, soft-stepping over heads and between spread legs, reciting numbers in the night, and a woman with a slate stood ready to mark the scene and take. Eric went to the corner and squeezed through a pair of warped boards that blocked the sidewalk. He stood inside the plywood framework breathing mortar and dust and removed his clothes. It took him a while to remember why his midsection smarted so badly. That's where he'd been frizzed by the stun gun, and how sensational she'd looked in the arc and strobe, his bodyguard in her armored vest. He felt a lingering sting, mid-dick, from the vodka she'd dribbled thereon.

He rolled his trousers tightly around the handgun and left all his clothes on the sidewalk. He felt his way in the dark, turning the corner and putting his shoulder to a board until he could see a fringe of light. He pushed slowly, hearing the board scrape the asphalt, and then sidled around the plywood and stepped into the street. He took ten baby steps, reaching the limits of the intersection and the border of fallen bodies.

He lay down among them. He felt the textural variation of slubs of chewing gum compressed by decades of traffic. He smelled the ground fumes, the oil leaks and rubbery skids, summers of hot tar. He lay on his back, head twisted, arm bent on chest. His body felt stupid here, a pearly froth of animal fat in some industrial waste. Out of one eye he could see the camera sweep the scene at a height of twenty feet. The master shot was still being prepared, he thought, while a woman with a hand-held camera prowled the area shooting digital video.

A high assistant called to a lesser, "Bobby, lock it up."

The street grew quiet in time. Voices died, the sense of outlying motion faded. He felt the presence of the bodies, all of them, the body breath, the heat and running blood, people unlike each other who were now alike, amassed, heaped in a way, alive and dead together. They were only extras in a crowd scene, told to be immobile, but the experience was a strong one, so total and open he could barely think outside it.

"Hello," someone said.

It was the person nearest him, a woman lying face-down, an arm extended, palm turned up. She had light brown hair, or brownish blond. Maybe it was fawn-colored. What is fawn? A grayish yellow-brown to a moderate reddish brown. Or sorrel. Sorrel sounded better.

"Are we supposed to be dead?"

174

"I don't know," he said.

"Nobody told us. I'm frustrated by that."

"Be dead then."

The position of her head forced her to speak into the blacktop, muffling her words.

"I assumed an awkward pose intentionally. Whatever has happened to us, I thought, probably happened without warning and I wanted to reflect that by individualizing my character. One entire arm is twisted painfully. But I wouldn't feel right if I changed position. Someone said that the financing has collapsed. Happened in seconds apparently. Money all gone. This is the last scene they're shooting before they suspend indefinitely. So there's no excuse for self-indulgence, is there?"

Didn't Elise have sorrel hair? He could not see the woman's face and she could not see his. But he'd spoken and she'd evidently heard him. If this was Elise, wouldn't she react to the sound of her husband's voice? But then why would she? It was not an interesting thing to do.

The rumble of a truck somewhere drummed on his spine.

"But I suspect we're not actually dead. Unless we're a cult," she said, "involved in a mass suicide, which I truly hope is not the case."

An amplified voice called, "Eyes closed, people. No sound or movement."

The crane shot commenced, camera slowly lowering, and he shut his eyes. Now that he was sightless among them, he saw the clustered bodies as the camera did, coldly. Were they pretending to be naked or were they naked? It was no longer clear to him. They were many shades of skin color but he saw them in black-and-white and he didn't know why. Maybe a scene such as this needed somber monochrome.

"Rolling," called another voice.

It tore his mind apart, trying to see them here and real, independent of the image on a screen in Oslo or Caracas. Or were those places indistinguishable from this one? But why ask these questions? Why see these things? They isolated him. They set him apart and this is not what he wanted. He wanted to be here among them, all-body, the tattoed, the hairy-assed, those who stank. He wanted to set himself in the middle of the intersection, among the old with their raised veins and body blotches and next to the dwarf with a bump on his head. He thought there were probably people here with wasting diseases, a few, undissuadable, skin flaking away. There were the young and strong. He was one of them. He was one of the morbidly obese, the tanned and fit and middle-aged. He thought of the children in the scrupulous beauty of their pretending, so formal and fine-boned. He was one. There were those with heads nested in the bodies of others, in breasts or armpits, for whatever sour allowance of shelter. He thought of those who lay faceup and wide-winged, open to the sky, genitals world-centered. There was a dark woman with a small red mark in the middle of her forehead, for auspiciousness. Was there a man with a missing limb,

176

brave stump knotted below the knee? How many bodies bearing surgical scars? And who is the girl in dreadlocks, folded into herself, nearly all of her lost in her hair, pink toes showing?

He wanted to look around but did not open his eyes until a long moment passed and a man's soft voice called, "Cut."

He took one step and extended an arm behind him. He felt her hand in his. She followed him into the boarded-off section of sidewalk, where he turned in the dark and kissed her, saying her name. She climbed his body and wrapped her legs around him and they made love there, man standing, woman astraddle, in the stone odor of demolition.

"I lost all your money," he told her.

He heard her laugh. He felt the spontaneous breath of it, the lap of humid air on his face. He'd forgotten the pleasure of her laugh, a smoky half cough, a cigarette laugh out of an old black-and-white movie.

"I lose things all the time," she said. "I lost my car this morning. Did we talk about this? I don't remember."

That's what this resembled, the next scene in the black-and-white film that was being screened in theaters worldwide, outside the script and beyond the need for refinancing. After the naked crowd, the two lovers in isolation, free of memory and time.

"First I stole the money, then I lost it."

She said laughingly, "Where?"

"In the market."

"But where?" she said. "Where does it go when you lose it?"

She licked his face and shinnied up his body and he could not remember where the money went. She ran her tongue over his eye and brow. He lifted her rhapsodically higher and mashed his face in her breasts. He felt them jump and hum.

"What do poets know about money? Love the world and trace it in a line of verse. Nothing but this," she said. "And this."

Here she put a hand to his head and took him, seized him by the hair, a thrilling fistful, drawing his head back and bending to kiss him, so prolonged and abandoned a kiss, with such heat of being, that he thought he knew her finally, his Elise, sighing, tonguing, biting his mouth, breathing muggy words and dying murmurs, whisper-kissing, babytalking, her body fused to his, legs girdling, buttocks hot in his hands.

The instant he knew he loved her, she slipped down his body and out of his arms. Then she wedged herself through the narrow opening in the boards and he watched her cross the street. Nothing moved out there. She was the lone stroke of motion, crew and extras gone, equipment gone, and she was cool and silvery slim and walking head-high, with technical precision, toward the last trailer in the service station, where she would find her clothes, dress quickly and disappear.

∗   ∗   ∗

He dressed in the dark. He felt the street grit, minutely coarse, studding his back and legs. He poked around for his socks but couldn't find them and went barefoot out to the street, carrying his shoes.

The last trailer was gone, intersection empty. He didn't sit with the driver this time. He wanted to be in the rear cabin of his cork-lined limousine, in bronzy light, alone in the flow of space, noting the lines and grains, the sweet transitions, this shape or texture modulated to that. The long interior had a thrust, a fluid motion rearward, and he smelled the leather around him and the red cedar paneling up front, used in the partition. He felt the marble underfoot, bone cold. He looked at the ceiling mural, a dark ink wash, semi-abstract, that showed the arrangement of the planets at the time of his birth, calculated to the hour, minute and second.

They crossed Eleventh Avenue into the car barrens. Old junked-up garages and ratty storefronts. Car repair, car wash, used cars. A sign reading Collision Inc. Stripped cars ranked on the sidewalk, tail ends to the street. It was the last block before the river, nonresidential, non-pedestrian, car lots fenced with razor wire, an area suited to his limo in its current condition. He put on his shoes. The car stopped near the entrance to an underground garage, where it would sit overnight and probably forever, or until it was evicted, scavenged and scrapped.

The wind came up. He stood in the street, near a derelict tenement, windows boarded, a padlocked iron door where the entrance used to be. He thought he'd like to get a can of gasoline and set fire to the car. Create a riverside pyre of wood, leather, rubber and electronic devices. It would be a great thing to do and see. This is Hell's Kitchen. Burn the car to a blackened scrap of dead metal, right here in the street. But he could not subject Ibrahim to such a spectacle.

The wind blew hard off the river. He and his driver met at the side of the car.

"Early morning you can see, right here, teams of men in white coveralls, they are washing the limousines. A marketplace of limos. Rags flying."

The two men embraced. Then Ibrahim got in the car and eased it down the ramp and into the garage. The steel grille came down. He would drive his own car out the exit on the next street and head on home.

The moon was mostly shadow, a waning crescent twenty-two days into its orbit, he estimated.

He stood in the street. There was nothing to do. He hadn't realized this could happen to him. The moment was empty of urgency and purpose. He hadn't planned on this. Where was the life he'd always led? There was nowhere he wanted to go, nothing to think about, no one waiting. How could he take a step in any direction if all directions were the same?

Then there was a shot. The sound flew in the wind. It was something, yes, an occurrence, but also nearly negligible, a hollow popping noise come and gone in a breath and carrying only the faintest intimation of danger. He didn't want to blow it out of proportion. Then another shot followed by a man's voice howling his name in a series of trochaic beats and at a cracked pitch that was more chilling than gunfire.

ERIC MICHAEL PACKER

So it was personal then. He remembered the gun in his belt. He took it in hand and prepared to sprint toward a couple of small dumpsters on the sidewalk behind him. There was shelter there, a blind from which to return fire. Instead he stood where he was, in the middle of the street, facing the padlocked building. Another shot sounded, barely, nearly lost in the ripping wind. It seemed to come from the third floor.

He looked at his gun. It was a snub-nosed revolver, small and blunt, with a wide trigger. He checked the cylinder, which held only five rounds. But he knew he would not be counting rounds.

He prepared to fire, eyes closed, visualizing his finger on the trigger, in tight detail, and also seeing the man in the street, himself, long-lensed, facing the dead tenement.

But there was something moving toward him, off his left shoulder. He opened his eyes. It was a man on a bike, a bike messenger, bare-chested, and he went swanning past, arms spread wide, and made a sweeping turn onto the West Side Highway, heading north along the terminals and piers.

Eric watched for a moment, semi-marveling at the sight. Then he turned and fired. He fired at the building itself, as a building. This was the target. It made every sense to him. It solved so many problems of who or whom.

The man fired back.

Why do people interpret gunshots as firecrackers going off or as cars backfiring? Because they aren't being hunted by a killer.

He approached the building. The padlocked door looked formidable, an iron-plated bulkhead. He thought of firing a shot into the lock for the sheer cinematic stupidity of the gesture. He knew there was another way in and out because the padlock could not be opened by someone inside the building. There was a gate to his left, some steps, an alley that was narrow and dog-shat, leading to a junked-up yard behind the building.

He pushed against an old misshapen door. His strength coach was a woman, Latvian. It gave way and he entered the building. The back hallway was swampish. A man lay dead or sleeping in the vestibule, if this is still a word, and he walked around the body and climbed two flights of stairs in the dim swinging light of a couple of strung bulbs.

The wind was blowing through the upper floors. There was fallen plaster on the landings and every sort of drift and silt and street debris. On the third floor he stepped over a number of unfinished meals in styrofoam trays, with neatly snuffed cigarettes worked to the nub. All the doors but one were gone and the wind came blowing through an unboarded window space. He liked that, the sound of wind knocking through the rooms and halls. He liked the two rats he saw moving toward the food nearby. The rats were good. The rats were fine and right, thematically sound.

He stood outside the one apartment that had a door. He stood with his back to the wall, shoulder nudging the jamb. He held the gun alongside his face, muzzle up, and looked straight ahead, into the windy hallway, not seeing things at maximum clarity but thinking into the moment.

Then he turned his head and looked at the gun, inches from his face.

He said, "I had a weapon I could talk to. Czech. But I threw it away. Or I'd be standing here trying to mimic Torval's voice so I could get the mechanism to respond. I happen to know the code. I can see myself standing here whispering *Nancy Babich Nancy Babich* in Torval's voice. I can say his name because he's dead. It was a weapons system, not a gun. You're a gun. I've seen a hundred situations like this. A man and a gun and a locked door. My mother used to take me to the movies. After my father died my mother took me to the movies. This is what we did as a parent and a child. And I saw two hundred situations where a man stands outside a locked room with a gun in his hand. My mother could tell you the actor's name in every case. He stands the way I'm standing, back to the wall. He is ramrod straight and he holds the gun the way I'm holding the gun, pointed up. Then he turns and kicks open the door. The door is always locked and he always kicks it open. These were old movies and new movies. Didn't matter. There was the door, there was the kick. She could tell you the actor's middle name, his marital history, the name of the rest home where his abandoned mother dozes in a chair. Always a single kick suffices. The door flies open at once. I left my sunglasses in the car or at the barbershop. I can see myself standing here whispering in vain. *Nancy Babich, you fucking cunt.* But then again, what? Once he said her name, maybe the firing system became operative for a specified period of time, or until every round was discharged. Because I can't imagine that you'd have to keep saying her name, rapid-firing in an alley at expressionless killers. These mothers with their movies in the afternoon. We used to sit in empty theaters where I'm telling her it's not possible to kick a door once and expect it to open. We're not talking about rickety screen doors in bad neighborhoods where the killing tends to be random type of movie. I was a kid and a little pedantic but I still maintain I had a point. He didn't say my name and I didn't say his. But now that he's dead, I can say his name. I know a little Czech, useful in restaurants and taxis, but I never studied the language. I could stand here and list the languages I've studied but what would be the point? I've never liked thinking back, going back in time, reviewing the day or the week or the life. To crush and gut. To eviscerate. Power works best when there's no memory attached. Ramrod straight. Whenever it happened as a parent and a child I used to tell her that whoever made this movie has no idea how hard it is to kick in a sturdy wooden door in real life. I left them at the barbershop, didn't I? Titanium and neoplastic. Because no matter what kind of movie we went to, it was a spy thriller, it was a western, it was a romance, it was a comedy, there was always a man with a gun outside a locked room who was ready to kick in the door. At first I didn't care about their relationship. But now I'm thinking they did amazing things because why else would he want to whisper her name to his handgun? Power works best when it makes no distinctions. Even science fiction, he stands there with his ray gun and kicks in a door. What's the difference between the protector and the assassin if both men are armed and hate me? I can see his dumb bulk on top of her. *Nancy Nancy Nancy.* Or he says her full name because this is what he tells his gun. I'm wondering where does she live, what does she think about when she rides the bus to work. I can stand here and see her coming out of the bathroom drying her hair. Women barefoot on parquet floors make me weak-kneed and crazy. I know I'm talking to a gun that can't respond but how does she undress when she undresses? I'm thinking did she meet him at her place or his place to do whatever they did. These mothers with their afternoons at the movies. We went to the movies because we were trying to learn how to be alone together. We were cold and lost and my father's soul was trying to find us, to settle itself in our bodies, not that I want or need your sympathy. I can picture her in the heat of sex, expressionless, because this is a Nancy Babich thing she does, blank-face. I say her name but not his. I used to be able to say his name but now I can't because I know what went on between them. I'm thinking is his picture in a frame on her dresser. How

185

many times do two people have to fuck before one of them deserves to die? I'm standing here enraged in my head. In other words how many times do I have to kill him? These mothers who accept the fiction of kicking in a door. What is a door? It's a movable structure, usually swinging on hinges, which closes off an entranceway and requires a tremendous and prolonged pounding before it can finally be forced open."

He stepped away from the wall and turned, positioning himself directly in front of the door. Then he kicked it, heel-first. It opened at once.

He entered shooting. He did not aim and fire. He just fired. Let it express itself.

The walls were down. This was the first thing he saw in the wobbly light. He was looking into a sizable space with wall rubble everywhere. He tried to spot the subject. There was a shredded sofa, unoccupied, with a stationary bike nearby. He saw a heavy metal desk, battleship vintage, covered with papers. He saw the remains of a kitchen and bathroom, with brutally empty spaces where major appliances had stood. There was a portable orange toilet from a construction site, seven feet tall, mud-smoked and dented. He saw a coffee table with an unlit candle in a saucer and a dozen coins scattered around an Mk.23 military pistol with a matte black finish and an overall length of nine and a half inches, equipped with a laser-aiming module.

The toilet door opened and a man came out. Eric fired again, indifferently, distracted by the man's appearance.

He was barefoot in jeans and T-shirt, with a bath towel over his head and shoulders, draped in the manner of a prayer shawl.

"What are you doing here?"

"That's not the question. The question," Eric said, "is yours to answer. Why do you want to kill me?"

"No, that's not the question. That's too easy to be the question. I want to kill you in order to count for something in my own life. See how easy?"

He walked over to the table and picked up the weapon. Then he sat on the sofa, hunched forward, half lost in the towel shroud.

"You're not a reflective man. I live consciously in my head," he said. "Give me a cigarette."

"Give me a drink."

"Do you recognize me?"

He was slight and unshaven and looked absurd trying to manage such a formidable weapon. The gun dominated him, even in the drama of the towel on his head.

"I can't see you clearly."

"Sit. We'll talk."

Eric didn't want to sit on the exercise bike. The confrontation would crumble into farce. He saw a molded plastic chair, the desk chair, and took it to the coffee table.

"Yes, I'd like that. Sit and talk," he said. "I've had a long day. Things and people. Time for a philosophical pause. Some reflection, yes."

The man fired a shot into the ceiling. It startled him. Not Eric; the other, the subject.

"You're not familiar with that weapon. I've fired that weapon. It's a serious weapon. Whereas this," he said, wagging the revolver in his hand. "I'm thinking of installing a shooting range in my apartment."

"Why not your office? Line them up and shoot them."

"You know the office. Is that right? You've been in the office."

"Tell me who you think I am."

The awfulness of his need, the half-pandering expectancy made it clear that Eric's next word, or the one after, could be his last. They faced each other across the table. It almost didn't occur to him that he could shoot first. Not that he knew whether there was a bullet left in the chamber.

He said, "I don't know. Who are you?"

The man took the towel off his head. This meant nothing to Eric. There was the high forehead. He saw the scarified hair, hanging in unwashed strips, thin and limp.

"Maybe if you told me your name."

"You wouldn't know my name."

"I know names more than faces. Tell me your name."

"Benno Levin."

"That's a phony name."

The man was a little stunned to hear this.

"It's phony. It's fake."

He was rattled and embarrassed.

"It's fake. It isn't real. But I think I recognize you now. You were at the cash machine outside a bank sometime after noon."

"You saw me."

"You looked familiar. I didn't know why. Maybe you used to work for me. Hate me. Want to kill me. Fine."

"Everything in our lives, yours and mine, has brought us to this moment."

"Fine. I could use a tall cold beer about now."

For all his haggardness, his stringiness, the ash of despair, there was a light in the subject's eye. He found encouragement in the thought that Eric had recognized him. Not recognized so much as simply seen. Seen and found linkage, faintly, on a crowded street. It was nearly lost inside the desperate bearing of the man, an attentiveness that wasn't feral or deadly.

"How old are you? I'm interested."

"Do you think people like me can't happen?"

"How old?"

"We happen. Forty-one."

"A prime number."

"But not an interesting one. Or did I turn forty-two, which is possible, because I don't keep track, because why should I?"

The wind was blowing through the halls. He looked chilled and put the towel back on his head, the ends falling over his shoulders.

"I have become an enigma to myself. So said Saint Augustine. And herein lies my sickness."

"That's a start. That's a crucial self-realization," Eric said.

"I'm not talking about myself. I'm talking about you.

Your whole waking life is a self-contradiction. That's why you're engineering your own downfall. Why are you here? That's the first thing I said to you when I came out of the toilet."

"I noticed the toilet. It's one of the first things I noticed. What happens to your waste?"

"There's a hole below the fixture. I knocked a hole in the floor. Then I positioned the toilet so that one hole fits over the other."

"Holes are interesting. There are books about holes."

"There are books about shit. But we want to know why you'd willingly enter a house where there's someone inside who's prepared to kill you."

"All right. Tell me. Why am I here?"

"You have to tell me. Some kind of unexpected failure. A shock to your self-esteem."

Eric thought about this. Across the table the man's head was lowered and he held the weapon between his knees, using both hands to grip it. The stance was patient and thoughtful.

"The yen. I couldn't figure out the yen."

"The yen."

"I couldn't chart the yen."

"So you brought everything down."

"The yen eluded me. This had never happened. I became halfhearted."

"This is because you have half a heart. Give me a cigarette."

"I don't smoke cigarettes."

190

"The huge ambition. The contempt. I can list the things. I can name the appetites, the people. Mistreat some, ignore some, persecute others. The self-totality. The lack of remorse. These are your gifts," he said sadly, without irony.

"What else?"

"Funny feeling in your bones."

"What?"

"Tell me if I'm wrong."

"What?"

"Intuition of early death."

"What else?"

"What else. Secret doubts. Doubts you could never acknowledge."

"You know some things."

"I know you smoke cigars. I know everything that's ever been said or written about you. I know what I see in your face, after years of study."

"You worked for me. Doing what?"

"Currency analysis. I worked on the baht."

"The baht is interesting."

"I loved the baht. But your system is so microtimed that I couldn't keep up with it. I couldn't find it. It's so infinitesimal. I began to hate my work, and you, and all the numbers on my screen, and every minute of my life."

"One hundred satang to the baht. What's your real name?"

"You wouldn't know it."

"Tell me your name."

He sat back and looked away. Telling his name seemed to strike him as an essential defeat, the most intimate failure of character and will, but also so inevitable there was no point resisting.

"Sheets. Richard Sheets."

"Means nothing to me."

He said these words into the face of Richard Sheets. *Means nothing to me.* He felt a trace of the old stale pleasure, dropping an offhand remark that makes a person feel worthless. So small and forgettable a thing that spins such disturbance.

"Tell me. Do you imagine that I stole ideas from you? Intellectual property."

"What does anyone imagine? A hundred things a minute. Whether I imagine a thing or not, it's real to me. I have syndromes where they're real, from Malaysia for example. The things I imagine become facts. They have the time and space of facts."

"You're forcing me to be reasonable. I don't like that."

"I have severe anxieties that my sex organ is receding into my body."

"But it's not."

"Shrinking into my abdomen."

"But it's not."

"Whether it is or not, I know it is."

"Show me."

"I don't have to look. There are folk beliefs. There are epidemics that happen. Men in the thousands, in real fear and pain."

He closed his eyes and fired a shot into the floorboards between his feet. He didn't open his eyes until the report stopped vibrating through the room.

"All right. People like you can happen. I understand this. I believe it. But not the violence. Not the gun. The gun is all wrong. You're not a violent man. Violence is meant to be real, based on real motives, on forces in the world that what. That make us want to defend ourselves or take aggressive action. The crime you want to commit is cheap imitation. It's a stale fantasy. People do it because other people do it. It's another syndrome, a thing you caught from others. It has no history."

"It's all history." He said, "The whole thing is history. You are foully and berserkly rich. Don't tell me about your charities."

"I have no charities."

"I know this."

"You don't resent the rich. That's not your sensibility."

"What's my sensibility?"

"Confusion. This is why you're unemployable."

"Why?"

"Because you want to kill people."

"That's not why I'm unemployable."

"Then why?"

"Because I stink. Smell me."

"Smell me," Eric said.

The subject thought about this.

"Even when you self-destruct, you want to fail more, lose more, die more than others, stink more than others. In the old tribes the chief who destroyed more of his property than the other chiefs was the most powerful."

"What else?"

"You have everything to live and die for. I have nothing and neither. That's another reason to kill you."

"Richard. Listen."

"I want to be known as Benno."

"You're unsettled because you feel you have no role, you have no place. But you have to ask yourself whose fault this is. Because in fact there's very little for you to hate in this society."

This made Benno laugh. His eyes went slightly wild and he looked around him, shaking and laughing. The laughter was mirthless and disturbing and the shaking increased. He had to put the weapon on the table so he could laugh and shake freely.

Eric said, "Think."

"Think."

"Violence needs a cause, a truth."

He was thinking of the bodyguard with the scarred face and air of close combat and the hard squat Slavic name, Danko, who'd fought in wars of ancestral blood. He was thinking of the Sikh with the missing finger, the driver he'd glimpsed when he shared a taxi with Elise, briefly, much earlier in the day, in the life, a time beyond memory nearly. He was thinking of Ibrahim Hamadou, his own driver, tortured for politics or religion or clan hatreds, a victim of rooted violence driven by the spirits of his enemies' forebears. He was even thinking of André Petrescu,

194

the pastry assassin, all those pies in the face and the blows he took in return.

Finally he thought of the burning man and imagined himself back at the scene, in Times Square, watching the body on fire, or in the body, was the body, looking out through gas and flame.

"There's nothing in the world but other people," Benno said.

He was having trouble speaking. The words exploded from his face, not loud so much as impulsive, blurted under stress.

"I had this thought one day. It was the thought of my life. I'm surrounded by other people. It's buy and sell. It's let's have lunch. I thought look at them and look at me. Light shines through me on the street. I'm what's the word, pervious to visible light."

He spread his arms wide.

"I thought all these other people. I thought how did they get to be who they are. It's banks and car parks. It's airline tickets in their computers. It's restaurants filled with people talking. It's people signing the merchant copy. It's people taking the merchant copy out of the leather folder and then signing it and separating the mer-chant copy from the customer copy and putting their credit card in their wallet. This alone could do it. It's people who have doctors who order tests for them. This alone," he said. "I'm helpless in their system that makes no sense to me. You wanted me to be a helpless robot soldier but all I could be was helpless."

195

Eric said, "No."

"It's women's shoes. It's all the names they have for shoes. It's all those people in the park behind the library, talking in the sun."

"No. Your crime has no conscience. You haven't been driven to do it by some oppressive social force. How I hate to be reasonable. You're not against the rich. Nobody's against the rich. Everybody's ten seconds from being rich. Or so everybody thought. No. Your crime is in your head. Another fool shooting up a diner because because."

He looked at the Mk.23 lying on the table.

"Bullets flying through the walls and floor. So useless and stupid," he said. "Even your weapon is a fantasy. What is it called?"

The subject looked hurt and betrayed.

"What's the attachment that abuts the trigger guard? What is it called? What does it do?"

"All right. I don't have the manhood to know these names. Men know these names. You have the experience of manhood. I can't think that far ahead. It's all I can do to be a person."

"Violence needs a burden, a purpose."

He pressed the muzzle of his gun, Eric did, against the palm of his left hand. He tried to think clearly. He thought of his chief of security flat on the asphalt, a second yet left in his life. He thought of others down the years, hazy and nameless. He felt an enormous remorseful awareness. It moved through him, called guilt, and strange how soft the trigger felt against his finger.

"What are you doing?"

"I don't know. Maybe nothing," he said.

He looked at Benno and squeezed the trigger. He realized the gun had one round left just about the time it fired, the briefest instant before, way too late to matter. The shot blew a hole in the middle of his hand.

He sat head down, out of ideas, and felt the pain. The hand went hot. It was all scald and flash. It seemed separate from the rest of him, pervertedly alive in its own little subplot. The fingers curled, middle finger twitching. He thought he could feel his pressure drop to shock level. Blood ran down both sides of the hand and a dark discoloration, a scorch mark, began to spread across the palm.

He shut his eyes against the pain. This made no sense but then it did in a way, intuitively, as a gesture of concentration, his direct involvement in the action of pain-reducing hormones.

The man across the table was folded over in his shroud. There seemed nothing left for him, anywhere, that might be worth doing or thinking about. Words fell out of the towel, or sounds, and he held one hand over the other, the bent hand pressing the still, the flat, the other hand, in identification and pity.

There was pain and there was suffering. He wasn't sure if he was suffering. He was sure Benno was suffering. Eric watched him apply a cold compress to the ravaged hand. It wasn't a compress and it wasn't cold but they agreed unspokenly to use this term for whatever palliative effect it might have.

The echo of the shot rang electrically through his forearm and wrist.

Benno knotted the compress caringly under the thumb, two handkerchiefs he'd spent some time spiraling together. At the lower forearm was a tourniquet he'd employed, a rag and pencil arrangement.

He went back to the sofa and studied Eric in pain.

"I think we should talk."

"We're talking. We've been talking."

"I feel I know you better than anyone knows you. I have uncanny insights, true or false. I used to watch you meditate, online. The face, the calm posture. I couldn't stop watching. You meditated for hours sometimes. All it did was send you deeper into your frozen heart. I watched every minute. I looked into you. I knew you. It was another reason to hate you, that you could sit in a cell and meditate and I could not. I had the cell all right. But I never had the fixation where I could train the mind, empty the mind, think one thought only. Then you shut down the site. When you shut down the site I was I don't know, dead, for a long time after."

There was a softness in the face, a regret at the mention of hate and coldheartedness. Eric wanted to respond. The pain was crushing him, making him smaller, he thought, reducing him in size, person and value. It wasn't the hand, it was the brain, but it was also the hand. The hand felt necrotic. He thought he could smell a million cells dying.

He wanted to say something. The wind blew through again, stronger now, stirring the dust of these toppled walls. There was something intriguing in the sound, wind indoors, the edge of something, the feel of something unprotected, an inside-outness, papers blowing through the halls, the door banging nearly shut, then swinging out again.

He said, "My prostate is asymmetrical."

His voice was barely audible. There was a pause that lasted half a minute. He felt the subject regard him carefully, the other. There was a sense of warmth, of human involvement.

"So is mine," Benno whispered.

They looked at each other. There was another pause.

"What does it mean?"

Benno nodded for a while. He was happy to sit there nodding.

"Nothing. It means nothing," he said. "It's harmless. A harmless variation. Nothing to worry about. Your age, why worry?"

Eric didn't think he'd ever known such relief, hearing these words from a man who shared his condition. He felt a sweep of well-being. An old woe gone, the kind of half-smothered knowledge that haunts the idlest thought. The hankies were blood-soaked. He felt a peace, a sweetness settle over him. He still held the gun in his good hand.

Benno sat nodding in his towel shroud.

He said, "You should have listened to your prostate."

"What?"

"You tried to predict movements in the yen by drawing on patterns from nature. Yes, of course. The mathematical properties of tree rings, sunflower seeds, the limbs of galactic spirals. I learned this with the baht. I loved the baht. I loved the cross-harmonies between nature and data. You taught me this. The way signals from a pulsar in deepest space follow classical number sequences, which in turn can describe the fluctuations of a given stock or currency. You showed me this. How market cycles can be interchangeable with the time cycles of grasshopper breeding, wheat harvesting. You made this form of analysis horribly and sadistically precise. But you forgot something along the way."

"What?"

"The importance of the lopsided, the thing that's skewed a little. You were looking for balance, beautiful balance, equal parts, equal sides. I know this. I know you. But you should have been tracking the yen in its tics and quirks. The little quirk. The misshape."

"The misweave."

"That's where the answer was, in your body, in your prostate."

Benno's gentle intelligence carried no trace of rebuke. He was probably right. There was something in what he said. It made hard sense, charting sense. Maybe he was turning out to be a worthy assassin after all.

He came around the table and lifted the handkerchiefs to look at the wound. They both looked. The hand was stiff, a crude cardboard part, veins shattered near the knuckles, going gray. Benno went to his desk and found some take-out paper napkins. He came back to the table, removing the bloody compress and placing napkins against the wound on both sides of the hand. Then he held his own hands apart, suspensefully, in a gesture of expectation. The napkins stuck to the wound. He stood and watched until he was satisfied that they'd remain in place.

They sat a while, facing each other. Time hung in the air. Benno leaned across the table and took the gun out of his hand.

"I still need to shoot you. I'm willing to discuss it. But there's no life for me unless I do this."

The pain was the world. The mind could not find a place outside it. He could hear the pain, staticky, in his hand and wrist. He closed his eyes again, briefly. He could feel himself contained in the dark but also just beyond it, on the lighted outer surface, the other side, belonged to both, feeling both, being himself and seeing himself.

Benno got up and began to pace. He was restless, shoeless, a gun in each hand, and he moved past the boarded windows at the north wall, stepping over electrical wiring and breastworks of plaster and wallboard.

"Don't you ever walk through the park behind the library and see all those people sitting in their little chairs and drinking at those tables on the terrace after work and hear their voices mingling in the air and want to kill them?"

Eric thought about this. He said, "No."

The man circled back past the remains of the kitchen, stopping to draw open a loose board and look out at the street. He said something into the night, then resumed his pacing. He was jittery, dance-walking, mumbling something audible this time, about a cigarette.

"I'm having my Korean panic attack. This is from holding in my anger all these years. But not anymore. You need to die no matter what."

"I could tell you my situation has changed in the course of the day."

"I have my syndromes, you have your complex. Icarus falling. You did it to yourself. Meltdown in the sun. You will plunge three and a half feet to your death. Not very heroic, is it?"

He was behind Eric now, and stationary, and breathing.

"Even if there's a fungus living between my toes that speaks to me. Even if a fungus told me to kill you, even then your death is justified because of where you stand on the earth. Even a parasite living in my brain. Even then. It relays messages to me from outer space. Even then the crime is real because you're a figure whose thoughts and acts affect everybody, people, everywhere. I have history, as you call it, on my side. You have to die for how you think and act. For your apartment and what you paid for it. For your daily medical checkups. This alone. Medical checkups every day. For how much you had and how much you lost, equally. No less for losing it than making it. For the limousine that displaces the air that people need to breathe in Bangladesh. This alone."

"Don't make me laugh."

"Don't make you laugh."

"You just made that up. You've never spent a minute of your life worrying about other people."

He could see the subject back down.

"All right. But the air you breathe. This alone. The thoughts you have."

"I could tell you my thoughts have evolved. My situation has changed. Would that matter? Maybe it shouldn't."

"It doesn't. But if I had a cigarette it might. One cigarette. One drag on one cigarette. I probably wouldn't have to shoot you."

"Is there a fungus that speaks to you? I'm serious. People hear things. They hear God."

He meant it. He was serious. He wanted to mean it, to hear anything the man might say, the whole shapeless narrative of his unraveling.

Benno came around the table and slumped on the sofa. He set the old revolver down and regarded his advanced weapon. Maybe it was advanced, maybe the military had scrapped it a day or two before. He pulled the towel lower on his face and aimed the pistol at Eric.

"Anyway you're already dead. You're like someone already dead. Like someone dead a hundred years. Many centuries dead. Kings dead. Royals in their pajamas eating mutton. Have I ever used the word mutton in my life? Came into my head, out of nowhere, mutton."

Eric regretted that he hadn't shot his dogs, his borzois, before leaving the apartment in the morning. Had it occurred to him to do this, in chill premonition? There was the shark in the thirty-foot tank lined with coral and sea moss, built into a wall of sandblasted glass blocks. He could have left orders for his aides to transport the shark to the Jersey shore and release it in the sea.

"I wanted you to heal me, to save me," Benno said.

His eyes shone beneath the hem of the towel. They were fixed on Eric, devastatingly. But it wasn't accusation he encountered. There was a plea in the eyes, retroactive, a hope and need in ruins.

"I wanted you to save me."

The voice had a terrible intimacy, a nearness of feeling and experience that Eric could not reciprocate. He felt sad for the man. What lonely devotedness and hatred and disappointment. The man knew him in ways no one ever had. He sat in collapse, gun pointed, but even the death he felt so necessary to his deliverance would do nothing, change nothing. Eric had failed this docile and friendless man, raging man, this lunatic, and would fail him again, and had to look away.

He looked at his watch. He happened to glance at his watch. There it was on his wrist, with a crocodile band, between the napkins stuck to his wound and the yellow pencil tourniquet. But the watch wasn't showing the time. There was an image, a face on the crystal, and it was his. This meant he'd activated the electron camera unintentionally, maybe when he shot himself. The camera was a device so microscopically refined it was almost pure information. It was almost metaphysics. It operated inside the watch body, collecting images in the immediate vicinity and displaying them on the crystal.

He rolled his arm and the face disappeared, replaced by a wire dangling overhead. A zoom shot followed, showing a beetle on the wire, in slow transit. He studied the thing, mouthparts and forewings, absorbed by its beauty, so detailed and gleaming. Then something changed around him. He didn't know what this could mean. What could this mean? He realized he'd known this feeling before, tenuously, not nearly so dense and textured, and the image on the screen was a body now, facedown on the floor.

He felt a blood hush, a pause in midbeing.

There were no bodies in plain sight. He thought of the body he'd seen earlier in the vestibule but how could the screen show the image of a thing that was outside camera range?

He looked at Benno, broody and distant.

Whose body and when? Have all the worlds conflated, all possible states become present at once?

He moved his arm, straightening and flexing, pointing the watch six different ways, but the body of a man, in long shot, remained on-screen. He looked up at the beetle moving in its specialized slowness down along the warps and seams of the wire, its old dumb leaf-eating arcadian pace, thinking it is in a tree, and he redirected the camera at the insect. But the prone body stayed on-screen.

He looked at Benno. He covered the watch with his good hand. He thought about his wife. He missed Elise and wanted to talk to her, tell her she was beautiful, lie, cheat on her, live with her in middling matrimony, having dinner parties and asking what the doctor said.

When he looked at the watch he saw the inside of an ambulance, with drip-feed devices and bouncing heads. The image lasted less than a second but the scene, the circumstance was familiar in some unearthly way. He covered the watch and looked at Benno, who rocked back and forth, a little mystically, muttering. He looked at the face of the watch. He saw a series of vaults, a wall of vaults or compartments, all sealed. Then he saw a vault slide open. He covered the watch. He looked up at the insect on the wire. When he looked at the watch again he saw an identification tag. It was a tag in long shot, fixed to a plastic wristband. He knew, he sensed that a zoom shot would follow. He thought of covering the watch but then did not. He saw the tag in tight close-up now and read the legend printed there. Male Z. He knew what this meant. He didn't know how he knew this. How do we know anything? How do we know the wall we're looking at is white? What is white? He covered the watch with his good hand. He knew that Male Z was the designation for the bodies of unidentified men in hospital morgues.

O shit I'm dead.

He'd always wanted to become quantum dust, transcending his body mass, the soft tissue over the bones, the muscle and fat. The idea was to live outside the given limits, in a chip, on a disk, as data, in whirl, in radiant spin, a consciousness saved from void.

The technology was imminent or not. It was semi-mythical. It was the natural next step. It would never happen. It is happening now, an evolutionary advance that needed only the practical mapping of the nervous system onto digital memory. It would be the master thrust of cyber-capital, to extend the human experience toward infinity as a medium for corporate growth and investment, for the accumulation of profits and vigorous reinvestment.

But his pain interfered with his immortality. It was crucial to his distinctiveness, too vital to be bypassed and not susceptible, he didn't think, to computer emulation. The things that made him who he was could hardly be identified much less converted to data, the things that lived and milled in his body, everywhere, random, riotous, billions of trillions, in the neurons and peptides, the throbbing temple vein, in the veer of his libidinous intellect. So much come and gone, this is who he was, the lost taste of milk licked from his mother's breast, the stuff he sneezes when he sneezes, this is him, and how a person becomes the reflection he sees in a dusty window when he walks by. He'd come to know himself, untranslatably, through his pain. He felt so tired now. His hard-gotten grip on the world, material things, great things, his memories true and false, the vague malaise of winter twilights, untransferable, the pale nights when his identity flattens for lack of sleep, the small wart he feels on his thigh every time he showers, all him, and how the soap he uses, the smell and feel of the concave bar make him who he is because he names the fragrance, amandine, and the hang of his cock, untransferable, and his strangely achy knee, the click in his knee when he bends it, all him, and so much else that's not convertible to some high sublime, the technology of mind-without-end.

He looked at the far wall, which was white. The insect was still on the wire. He looked at the insect coming down the dangling wire. Then he took his good hand off the watchface. He looked at the watch. The legend remained on-screen, reading Male Z.

There was a trace of enzyme left, the old biochemistry of the ego, his saturated self. He imagined Kendra Hays, his bodyguard and lover, washing his viscera in palm wine in a ceremony of embalming. She had the face for it, the bone structure and skin color, the tapered planes. It was a face from a wall painting in some mortuary temple buried in sand for four thousand years, with dog-headed gods in attendance.

He thought of his chief of finance and touchless lover, Jane Melman, masturbating quietly in the last row of the funeral chapel, in a dark blue dress with a cinched waist, during the whispery dimness of the vigil.

There was something else to consider, that he'd married when he'd married in order to have a widow to leave behind. He imagined his wife, his widow, shaving her head, perhaps, in response to his death, and choosing to wear black for a year, and watching the burial in isolated desert terrain, from a distance, with her mother and the media.

He wanted to be buried in his nuclear bomber, his Blackjack A. Not buried but cremated, conflagrated, but buried as well. He wanted to be solarized. He wanted the plane flown by remote control with his embalmed body aboard, suit, tie and turban, and the bodies of his dead dogs, his tall silky Russian wolfhounds, reaching maximum altitude and leveling at supersonic dash speed and then sent plunging into the sand, fireballed one and all, leaving a work of land art, scorched earth art that would interact with the desert and be held in perpetual trust under the auspices of his dealer and executor, Didi Fancher, and longtime lover, for the respectful contemplation of pre-approved groups and enlightened individuals under exempt-status section 501(c)(3) of the U.S. Internal Revenue Code.

What did the doctor say?

It's fine, it's nothing, it's normal.

Maybe he didn't want that life after all, starting over broke, hailing a cab in a busy intersection filled with jockeying junior executives, arms aloft, bodies smartly spinning to cover every compass point. What did he want that was not posthumous? He stared into space. He understood what was missing, the predatory impulse, the sense of large excitation that drove him through his days, the sheer and reeling need to be.

His murderer, Richard Sheets, sits facing him. He has lost interest in the man. His hand contains the pain of his life, all of it, emotional and other, and he closes his eyes one more time. This is not the end. He is dead inside the crystal of his watch but still alive in original space, waiting for the shot to sound.

Don DeLillo, the author of thirteen novels, including *White Noise* and *Libra,* has won many honors in this country and abroad, including the National Book Award, the *Irish Times* International Fiction Prize, the Jerusalem Prize for his complete body of work and the Howells Medal of the American Academy of Arts and Letters for his novel *Underworld.* His last novel was *The Body Artist.*